# A Fabricated Mexican

## Rick P. Rivera

Público Press
Houston, Texas
1995

This volume is made possible through grants from the National Endowment for the Arts (a federal agency), the Lila Wallace-Reader's Digest Fund, and the Andrew W. Mellon Foundation.

*Recovering the past, creating the future*

Arte Público Press
University of Houston
452 Cullen Performance Hall
Houston, Texas 77204-2004

Cover design by James F. Brisson

Rivera, Rick P.
   A fabricated Mexican / by Rick P. Rivera.
      p.   cm.
   ISBN 1-55885-130-5
I. Title.
PS3568.I8314F3   1995
813'.54—dc20                                  94-33576
                                               CIP

4 5 6 7 8 9 0 1          11 10 9 8 7 6 5 4

*Para mi esposa*, Jeannine Marie, *mi suegra*, Rosalie Marie,
*y también para mis hermanos*, Domingo, Angelica, Antonio,
René, Apolonio, *y* Margarita.

*Pero más que todo, para mi mamá,* Consuelo L. Luna

―――――――――――

This is a work of fiction. Characters, dialogues, incidents, and places are fabrications of the author's imagination and are not to be construed as real. Any resemblance to actual persons or events, living or dead, *es pura casualidad.*

# A Fabricated Mexican

## 1

According to my mother, I was conceived in a plum orchard. How I know this bit of husbandry is due to my mother's attempt to explain to me the gap in years between myself and the rest of my many brothers and sisters.

"Well, your daddy was drunk one night, and he want to make love," she explained to me in her rendition of English. "I didn't want to, but you know how you mens are. When they want something, it's their doing." She continued, "We was living on Martino's farm in San Jose, in them little shacks your daddy help build. You know, there was only one room and there was eight of us before you was born, so we had to go to the fields when we want to be alone."

"Yes," I said, "I remember Martino's, I think. There were three rooms connected, and we were on one end. You could look through the cracks in the walls and see the family next door. And wasn't there a little stove, and a bed, and a television with aluminum-foil rabbit ears?" I reached back through the furrows of my mind, trying to remember my earliest childhood events and surroundings.

"That's right," she answered. She looked at me with skepticism, wondering if I actually remembered what I was recounting, or if I was repeating something I had heard one of my older siblings say.

"And didn't Mónica and I sleep in the bed with you and dad? And everybody else slept on the floor?"

My mother looked at me with suspicion, and her face became ripe with embarrassment. "Yes, we was very poor then. Everybody had to work."

"And didn't I used to go with you to pick plums because that was how you baby-sat me?"

"Yes," she said, "And do you remember your plum bucket?"

"Yes, I do!" I replied as I grew excited from the sprouting memories I had once thought were buried so deep. "It was a plastic lard bucket."

"That's right, and you use to pretend you was working so hard just like us. You was like a little *tacuache*, a little possum, with your big eyes. And we use to call you *ojos de tacuache* and you would start crying and say, 'I'm not a ca-ca-uache.' You was so *curioso*."

Her eyes grew misty from the melancholy of remembering. She continued, "And at night, your daddy and Hilario, and Roberto, and Andrés, and Ignacio would go work in the ovens drying the plums to turn them into prunes. And Andrés, he was the boss of everybody." She leaned back in her chair and lifted her head slightly as a trace of pride eased the pain brought on by these memories.

"Why was Andrés the boss?" I asked. "He wasn't even the oldest."

"Because he was such a good worker and he speak both languages," she explained. "And you know how mean he was. The other workers did what he said."

"Even dad?"

"Well, Andrés knew your daddy and he knew he had to respect him. Besides, your daddy was a good worker, too. We all was. That's why we got to live on the farm for as long as we wanted to."

"And didn't we used to go to Martino's big house and watch television sometimes?" I asked. And before my mother could answer, I blurted out, "Martino liked us, huh?"

"Oh, yesss," she said as she maintained her prideful posture. "Do you remember one of Martino's daughters was in love with Bobby?" she said with the tone of one who asks a trick question. She continued, knowing that she had exceeded the limits of my memory. "Well, first, she was in love with Hilario, then she find out he wanted to go in the Air Force, and Roberto wanted to be a doctor, so she fell in love with your brother Bobby. Womens can be that way," she warned.

"What about Beatrice?" I asked, "I don't remember her there."

"No, no, your sister was always in love with somebody. I knew she would get married early and leave the family."

"And wasn't Nacho always getting yelled at?" I probed.

"*Ay*, that Nacho, he was the *huevon* of the family and the most troublemaker." She chuckled as she shook her head from side to side. "He has always been a *gato*." She laughed and told me more about my birth. "When you was born, he told everybody that none of us know I was pregnant because I always had a big belly. He said I just cames home one day and you was there with me, and I wasn't so big as I used to be. And then he started that rumor that you was adopted."

We laughed together for a few moments. Silently, we both reached back to retrieve more memories from years when I was too young to fully remember. My mother began to cry softly as tears wet the brown brown skin of her face.

"It was very tough," she said with a heavy sigh.

# 2

After all these years, I am still amazed that I really don't know who this woman is. None of us do. My six brothers and sisters have conflicting fictions of where Chelo is from, but we agree that if we could just pinpoint an exact geographical moment of being, we could start to figure our mother out.

They are strange, the stories that we know about her. When there is a family reunion, inevitably, my mother's seven grown children sit around a table and begin the inquisition. A couple of popular theories have become family lore, but the evidence we have dredged up is purely circumstantial and vigorously denied by the woman of the house.

One of my brothers once claimed to have traced her roots to the city of El Tigre in the state of Chihuahua. "Not true!" she decried. And we still persist accusingly that yes, it must be true! "That's why your nickname is *La Tigresa.*"

"My nickname is *La Tigresa* because of my green eyes and because when we worked in the fields, I was so mean and bossy with everyone," she retorted. "Don't be so hard-headed."

Another family study showed her coming from Reynosa, from the other side of the Rio Bravo, but on the Mexican side to be sure. Most of us liked this theory. It made more sense and is more romantic for us when we consider that our father came from Burgos, Tamaulipas, which is just south of there. Since he died of a harrowed heart and a poisoned mind at an early stage in my life, we cannot appeal to him for a patriarchal version.

But my mother is in denial when it comes to admitting to Mexican roots, and the debates about her origins usually begin with her claiming, steadfastly, that she was born in Texas.

"Well, where in Texas?" we want to know.

And one time she will say Pharr, Texas; another time Donna. Falfurrias pops up as an answer, as do Cotulla, Catarina, and Quemado. The sub-text in whatever she answers is that she is from *here*, the *Estados Unidos* side of the river, and the underlying meaning of her claim is: "you can't prove otherwise." We have more modern, educated theories to which my mother does not pay much attention or cares to understand. "She's an illegal alien!" one brother will joke. "No, she's a space alien!" another will tease. And she will look at us with Cleopatra eyes holding a seductive secret that she has kept ever since any of us children can recall.

The other stories that we know about our mother reveal that her character and temperament have been consistent with what we later experienced ourselves first-hand. And I am thinking of the times when we didn't work fast enough in the fields and farmlands of lush California valleys, and she brought us in line with a slap of her hand or a threatening fist.

"Mom, I still don't believe that story about your dad and the turtle," my sister Beatrice said with skepticism.

"Yeah, I don't either," Andrés agreed, his chin so tight it pushed his lips up to meet his nose and formed a disbelieving scowl.

"Oh, but it's true," she said. "You kids don't believe nothing I tell you." She twisted a paper napkin with her busy hands and fleetingly looked at each one of us as she surveyed those who were seated at her kitchen table. "We was picking cotton in Texas and—"

"Where in Texas?" the smart-aleck brother, Nacho, asked, and we all laughed, except my mother.

"*Pues,* never mind. If you all are going to make fun of me, I won't tell you nothing."

We all apologized in turn and sat straight in our chairs with our hands dutifully folded in front of us on the table to indicate that we would be good.

"My father founds a *tortuga* once when we was picking cotton. And I wanted that *tortuga* for a pet. I cried and cried all day for that *pobre animal* while I picked cotton. My daddy put it in a sack, and after we finished that day, he butchered it to make soup. Then he beat me because I was crying all day for something silly like a *tortuga,* even though I picked my share of cotton. That day I made a *promesa* to myself that when I had my own home, I would have *tortugas* for pets."

She looked at us more forcefully as if to measure the impact and pathos of her story.

"Did you eat the soup?" my other sister, Mónica, asked.

"Why do you ask such a *tonta* question like that?" my mother countered with indignation. Her story cheapened by such a query.

"Well, did you?" my brother Roberto asked, pressing for an answer.

"Of course I eat the soup!" my mother snapped. "My daddy would probably have given me another beating if I didn't."

"Do you ever think about eating those guys?" Nacho teased as he pointed to the backyard where my mother's two tortoises, *Algodón* and *Lento,* were luxuriating in the cool green grass.

"You leave my turtles alone," my mother warned, "or I make soup out of your *huevos, hombre.* And what kind of man would you be with no balls?" And she laughed at us as we shook our heads in disgust at her vulgarity. She rose from the table and went to the window to check on her pets, as if the thought of them being a meal might have cursed them.

"Look at them," she beamed. "They're so *curioso.* You see how I paint them?"

We looked at each other curiously and realized that we haven't paid much attention to my mother's tortoises. "What do you mean 'paint them?'" a few of us asked in harmony.

"Look," she said, pointing outside. And as *Algodón* and *Lento* slowly made their way towards the little garden that my mother has planted just for them, she smiled proudly as if to admire a private victory. Each tortoise had a fluorescent orange dot that covered a substantial portion of its shell.

"What in the hell did you do that for?" my brother Hilario, the serious one, asked.

And my mother, still appreciating her creeping creatures, informed us that, "I did that so I can see them at night when I need to check on them. The dots shine in the dark, and I know where they are and if they are okay. Last week it was raining so hard I was worried about them, and I didn't know where they were or if they had drowned." She was proud of her ingenuity in spite of our laughter.

We returned to the table knowing that more would be shared in the way of family tales. As I am the youngest by

many years—and at times because of my lack of knowledge of
family history, the most ingenuous—I wanted to know about
an incident that involved me. "Mom, tell us about the burning
car," I requested.

Hilario kicked at me under the table as an indication that
I had crossed a sensitive line. My mother, aware of this, lifted
her head with dignity to defy any emotions that might surface
to break her down. "I tell you all about it," she said in a men-
acing tone.

"It was about twenty-five years ago when you, Ricky, was
only three years old."

"I remember," I said. "I still remember seeing the car on
fire."

My mother looked at me with her head turned slightly
away from me and her eyebrows slanting downward in an
expression that questioned my comment. "You was too young
to remember."

"Yeah, you was too young to remember," mimicked Beatrice.

"No, really, I remember. As we drove away, you told me
to look at the pretty fire."

"¡Fíjase nomás! Maybe you do remember a little bit," my
mother relented. "Anyway, it was very late at night and all of
you kids was asleep. I knew good and well that *desgraciado*
would not come home again when he was supposed to. He had
been doing this to me for too many times now and I was *bien*
fed up with it...."

We had heard this story before. In this one, my mother
seldom deviated from the hard facts. She even kept as evidence, should anyone of us not believe *nothing* she tells us,
the newspaper article that gave a report of the burning car on
the day following the incident. For many days immediately
after the incendiary event, she held her ground as she firmly
denied any knowledge of who would do such a thing and why.
She had her baby boy in her arms and her other children
flocked around her as she answered stern questions from suspecting investigators who knew more than they were letting
on. During the questioning, the implied scenario was that she
was a busy, hard-working woman who had many young ones
to support. And just because the charred vehicle had belonged
to her husband, this fact did not necessarily mean that she
knew more than he allowed her to know.

"*No, no se,*" she would answer to investigators' questions offering the Mexican version of the Fifth Amendment. "I was taking care of too much childrens to know anything," she would throw in as a rhetorical ploy that histrionically indicated a limited knowledge of English—which also meant a limited knowledge of anything outside of a woman's assigned domain.

"...So on the last night that I was going to give your daddy one more chance to get home on time, he doesn't came home," she continued. "I already knew who the woman was, and he knew I knew who she was, and that *cantinera* knew I knew who she was, but the two of them still wanted to make me feel like a dog and rub my face in it. That night, when he was supposed to be home, and everybody was sleeping, I took Ricardito to the old car we had and laid him down on the front seat. In the garage, I had a can of gasoline that I was saving especially for this day. We drove to Lupita's house, and I parked across the street from where your daddy's brand new red Ford was parked."

She interrupted her story to reminisce with a bitter editorial: "He thought he was such a big shot in that car. He would go everywhere by hisself in *his* red Ford showing off, and he would leave me with that old station wagon that doesn't have a back seat." She thought for another moment and then shrugged her shoulders, "Oh, well, I didn't never had a license anyway."

Her fingers lightly traced the patterns of swirls and circles on the tablecloth as she stared down and seemingly through the table. "Just when I parked the car, you wake up," she said, her right hand leaving the patterns on the tablecloth and pointing a finger at me. "And of course, you started crying because you didn't know where you was. I told you to watch what your *mamá* was going to do, but I didn't never think you was going to remember it."

But I recalled much more of it than my mother had ever expected. I remembered her quickly and stealthily walking around my father's shiny, new, sexy red Ford and splashing gasoline on the hood, the fenders, the doors, the trunk, and the roof until only weak ejaculations of gasoline spit from her emptying can. She took a couple of steps back, lit a cigarette, and threw it on the vehicle. As it burst into flames, she walked a straight line to her old single-seated station wagon, not looking back at the conflagration. She gently placed the gasoline can behind the front seat and quietly closed the car door. As she drove away, she said, "Look at the pretty fire *m'ijo.*"

And I did look at the pretty fire. I stood on the front seat and looked at the fire, first through the side windows of the station wagon and then through the back window as we slowly drove away from the bursting glow. *"Méndigo,"* she hissed as she held the steering wheel tightly, eyes lasered on the black road in front of her, and a slight, satisfying smile punctuating her determined face.

"Wow, Mom! You're nuts!" Nacho said after hearing the story yet again, and as all of us—brothers, sisters, cousins, in-laws, nephews and nieces who were old enough to understand—still amazed at the story of the burning car.

There was so much we knew about her and her ways. Her determination, her purpose, her willingness to confront and challenge bosses who called us dirty Mexicans, and teachers who told us we were stupid, neighbors who scoffed at our poverty, and husbands who didn't help to resolve matters. And to this day, I still wonder who this woman is.

# 3

I didn't know my father for very long. His life ended as mine was beginning. What I do remember most about him was the little word game we played with each other whenever he was taking care of me. The rest of the family was attending school or working, or both. I was too young for school, and since my father worked nights, he watched me during the day while my mother was at her job.

I did the usual things that little preschool-aged boys do by themselves. I played with my toys. I wandered around the yard. I chased the dog, and the dog chased me. And all the time, I kept an eye and an ear sighted and tuned to my father's movements as he repaired things around the house.

Quite often as I was blissfully playing by myself, I would think that I heard my father calling me. Since he only spoke Spanish, and at the time so did I, I would respond to his call, imagined or otherwise, by saying, "*¿Papá, me quieres?*" What I thought I was asking, and I was, was "Papa, do you want me?"

He would respond by spreading his arms wide and saying, "*Ay, m'ijito, te quiero mucho.*" And he would pick me up and hug and kiss me and dance a little dance. We laughed together as I would playfully slap at his head and he would bury his face in my soft baby's belly and tickle me with his moustache.

The verb *querer* means to want. It also means to love. *Amar* also means to love, but in a more romantic sense. You could say, *Te quiero*, to mean I love you. But to say *Te amo* is much more tumescent and torrid with the feelings that lovers share.

The verb *llamar* means to call. I guess I should have asked, "*¿Papá, me llamas?*" or "*¿Papá, me estás llamando?*" But it always came out with *querer*.

I was six years old when my father died. I was thirty-six when I found out the details. I was always aware of the manner in which he died, even at six. Everybody knew. My neighborhood. My friends. My teachers. Their friends.

I sat on the curb with my best friend Gerald. Across the street at my house, people were arriving with food and prayers. "Your father's dead," Gerald said with a matter-of-fact calm.

"Yeah," I said with equal composure, "but he'll be back."

"How can he be back if he's dead?" Gerald asked with a curious puzzlement.

"Because God is going to bring him back, that's how."

God never did bring my father back. And for years thereafter, I would wonder what happened. As I got older, my mother would explain to me that, "Your father found out he had cancer and he needed to have an operation. He did not want to live that way."

"So he killed himself?" I would ask with extreme confusion.

During my troubled years as a teenager, I refused to believe my mother's story. It was during those years and into my early twenties that I began to ask her if my dad had not left me a note or something. "No, he just left, and we found him a few days later," she would explain, never looking at me as she said this. And I would later conclude that there couldn't be a note because illiterate people seldom write things down.

I remember the day one of my brothers found his body. It was in a field of tall grass not far from our house. My brothers, who together or alone, were a rough bunch, sat in the living room sobbing dolorously.

My father looked so handsome in his suit as he lay in his casket. He did not look like the raging alcoholic that he had been. His body did not look like a .38 caliber bullet had ripped through his heart and lungs. He did not look like a man who had been pained by a plaintive existence. I think it was one of the few times that he ever wore a suit.

The first time I saw the guy, I thought to myself, "What an ugly old bird." But, he caught me by surprise as he introduced himself, "Ramón del Sol." He extended his hand and shook mine like one man greeting another.

I was nine years old when my mother announced to her children that she would be marrying this skinny Mexican man who looked Asian.

"Not without our permission," my brother Andrés, the real mean one, mandated.

"*Cómo que*, not without your permission?" my mother asked in a haughty and disbelieving tone. As she protested, with an increasing pitch in her voice, her tirade was interrupted as my brother explained, "He has to come and ask us, and then we will decide."

My mother stepped close to Andrés. Her left hand was on her hip and her other hand held the rolling pin that she often used to reinforce her point. Her face was only inches from his; the rest of the gang was around, alert, and anticipating some action.

"My money's on Mom," Nacho joked as he pierced Roberto's ribs with an elbow.

"Shut up, Nacho!" Andrés ordered, "Or I'll take you outside and show you what's what."

"Why take me outside?" scoffed Nacho. "Are you afraid to ruin our beautiful French provincial furniture?" Andrés lunged at Nacho, and Hilario and Bobby formed a human barrier to deflect the angry fists.

"Stop it!" my mother screamed. "If you *brutos* think you can tell me how to live, you're *bien loco*. You're not going to tell me who I can marry. You're all still young—Nacho is only seventeen. You don't know nothing about life—," and her declaration of independence suddenly ended. She thought for a moment as the atmosphere remained tense. She started again, but with a threatening calm. "Okay, look. I let you meet him and talk to him, but, if you don't treat this man with respect, *adiós*. I have my life, too."

Andrés stared down at the fierce detractor.

"Marquis de Queensberry rules?" asked Nacho as the older boys except Andrés, laughed.

"One of these days you are going to regret what you say in front of me," Andrés promised his younger brother.

Nacho lashed back. "You don't think I already regret? You knocked out four of my front teeth and now I walk around with these cheap fake ones. George Washington had better teeth than mine!" This time, they leaped at one another. The scuffle only lasted seconds as my sisters screamed, my other brothers tried to separate the combatants, and my mother yelled for order.

"*¡Animales!*" she said as she shook her head in disbelief.

Before the summit meeting was to begin, and before Ramón del Sol showed up, the women were banished from the house. As the youngest, I was relegated to my room. Interested in who this man was and how he would hold up to Andrés, I stealthily crept into the hallway to watch the impending interrogation.

He was dressed in the finery of a proud executive. He had on a three-piece suit, a very dapper-looking overcoat, black leather gloves, a hat, and black dress shoes. He confidently knocked on the door. Andrés answered the door wearing his patented silent stare.

Ramón removed his hat and began in Spanish, "Andrés Coronado? Good afternoon, my name is Ramón del Sol. I want to discuss with you the possibility of marrying your mother."

"What?" Andrés asked as he stood in the doorway, his chest puffed like a rooster about to define the pecking order.

"My name is Raymond del Sol, and I here to talk to you about marry with you *mamá*," he replied this time in English without retreating. His head bobbed a little, as one who is involved in important negotiations.

"Come in," Andrés ordered.

On the couch sat the two oldest boys, Hilario and Bobby. On each armrest of the couch sat a can of beer. Next to Bobby, kneeling on the floor, was Nacho, who periodically drank from the beer that Bobby ignored. "Would you like a beer?" Bobby politely asked as he stood to greet Ramón.

Nacho, impressed with Bobby's manners, blurted out, "Bobby's going to be a doctor!"

Ramón, still standing, replied, "*¡Ah, qué bueno!* that's good."

"Shut up, Nacho!" Andrés ordered. And Nacho saluted like a Nazi.

"May I sit down?" Ramón asked.

"Go ahead," replied Andrés, and while still standing, he started in like a prosecuting attorney, "What do want with my mother?"

Ramón, alert but calm, looked up at Andrés and then ran his look to the other boys. "*Bueno,*" he started slowly, "I wish to marry with you *mamá.* I am alone and I have my own property. My children are married and have moved away. I been working at the Clorox warehouse for twenty-five years. I have two pickup trucks, many tools, and I know how to fix many-thing." Bobby looked at Ramón with admiration and respect as the skinny man gave a straightforward, unflinching testi-mony. He continued, "I retire pretty soon, and I hope me and you *mamá* can enjoy life sometimes instead of working *como burros.* You *mamá* have a very hard life; she work hard all her life, and me, too."

Andrés looked at him as a boxer stares at his opponent right before the fight begins. "And where are you going to live?" he demanded.

"Where you want us to live?" Ramón quickly responded, his gaze locked into Andrés' bullying stare. "We can live here, and I sell my property. Or we can live in my property. *Como tú quieras.*"

The rivals continued staring at each other. "Get him a beer," Andrés ordered to no one in particular. Andrés finally offered his hand to Ramón and said, "Andrés Coronado, pleased to meet you."

Ramón smiled and replied, "*Mucho gusto.*"

Bobby brought the beer and patted Ramón on the shoul-der. Hilario leaned forward and offered his hand. "Mom's going to get married!" exclaimed Nacho, and he shrank back into his kneeling form as Andrés looked at him with eyes that pledged more pain.

"Look, Ramón," Andrés began, "we are very concerned for our mother. I think you know how our dad died. And we don't want her to go through anything like that again." Andrés' tone had dramatically changed and genuine concern was now emanating from what he said. "We don't all live here. Me, Hilario, Beatrice, and Bobby have our own places. I work for Standard Oil. Nacho is only`around when he's not in juvi. Most of the time it's just our mom, Mónica, and Ricky, so we can't keep an eye on her all of the time like we used to." Andrés stopped to study Ramón's reaction. Ramón looked back and nodded his head in understanding.

"When do you plan on getting married?" asked Bobby.

"*Pues, prontito*," replied Ramón. "We go to *mi tierra* for our honeymoon."

"Where's your *tierra*?" asked Hilario, who up to this point had been more concerned with his beer and the date he had later that night.

"Durango, Santa Maria del Valle," answered Ramón. "Do you know Durango?"

"No, we just know Tijuana," replied Nacho.

Andrés proudly offered, "That's where I had my Impala tuck-and-rolled."

"Oh, is that you Impala?" Ramón asked, "Very clean. Do you use much oil?"

"No, it's pretty good."

"Hey, Ramón," Bobby began, "you said you can fix anything. Can you fix that hole in the wall?" And he pointed to a jaggedly round hole about five and a half feet from the floor. Hilario got up to fetch more beer, and Nacho offered, "That's where Andrés shoved my head through the wall."

Ramón stared at Nacho to see if he was kidding, and then he looked at Andrés, whose face grew red from the inspection. "*Pues claro que* yes," he started, "I told you I can fix manything. You should see my house. I build it myself, everything."

And the discussion turned to fixing things around the battle-scarred house, cars and upholstery, and preliminary wedding details.

"When Mom gets home, we'll tell her the news," Andrés said as his eyes sparkled with the effect of a few beers and the thought of having conducted a successful meeting.

I stood there with my right leg self-consciously crossed over my left leg. My stiff, new baseball mitt barely maintained its loose fit on my left hand, and my shoulders drooped as I waited my turn.

"Get ready," a young coach called out as he threw a baseball into the air and took a confident, crisp swing at it. The ball shot past me and into the outfield. "You gotta put your glove down, son," he offered, "and uncross your legs. Let's try it again." I obeyed him and responded by bending forward slightly and turning the palm of my glove toward the batter, striking the pose of a confused chimp. Another ground ball whizzed by me as I made a half-hearted attempt to snare it. "Don't be afraid of the ball," the young coach further advised, "you gotta get in front of it."

"Like this, Ricky," my friend, Jesse Colmenares, demonstrated as he punched his right fist into his well-worn glove and maintained the pose of an aggressive infielder inviting the ball to penetrate his body. I mimicked him and reacted after the fact as the next ball missiled between my legs.

The square piece of paper safety-pinned to the front of my shirt indicated my number as a candidate for Little League.

"Number 34 needs to wake up," said one observant coach to his assistant. "The kid next to him sure looks good though. A good fielder and a strong arm. What's his name?"

"Colmenares, J.," the assistant answered in an almost whispering voice as he studied a clipboard. "We should try to pick him early; he's only a ten-year old."

As the rest of the young athletes took their turns at fielding ground balls and throwing to first base, Jesse surreptitiously moved closer to me, being careful not to break any rules. He held his gloved hand up to the side of his face in an effort to hide his communicating lips and imitated what he had seen the pros do.

"Stay in front of the ball, Ricky, and keep your eye on it all the way into your glove. Take your time when you throw to first, there's nobody running anyway, they just want to see how good you can field and what kind of arm you got."

I looked at my companion with a face that signaled resignation. Jesse understood the look by now, and even though we were the same age, he knew more things and had more confidence. He slapped me on the butt with his ungloved hand and sidled back to his place in the infield.

"Riiii-ckyyyy Cor-o-na-doooo," the stabbing voice taunted, "What are *you* doing here? You ain't gonna make it." It was Danny Méndez, an eleven-year old star and future pitcher for the Los Angeles Dodgers, at least by his own admission.

"I know—," I began. But before I could explain to him that my mother made me try out for Little League, and that I would rather be at home playing with my dog or reading, Jesse looked over and casually said, "Shut up, Danny. Nobody asked you."

"Well, I'm tellin' you!" Danny sneered. "Anyway, what are you going to do about it, Jeee-suuus?" Jesse looked at Danny and smiled a sneaky smile while saying nothing.

"Get ready, 34!" the coach yelled. The ball took two skipping bounces before it stung my chest and came to rest at my feet. I stared at it like it was a foreign and unfamiliar object.

"Pick it up! Pick it up and throw to first, Ricky!" Jesse shouted as if I was blowing the final game of the World Series. I picked up the ball and threw it to first. The ball traveled with the velocity of a butterfly enjoying its desultory flight.

"Sssssssss," Danny hissed, "you're attracting flies Ricky," and he walked off to join a group of other Little League stars and future big leaguers.

"Okay, 21, this is to you," the hitting coach warned, and he lashed a sizzling grounder to Jesse's left. Jesse shuffled laterally to meet the shooting spheroid and, fielding the ball immaculately, threw an imaginary runner out at first.

"Okay, guys, line up in the outfield for fly balls," a coach ordered.

"This is where you can show them that you're a good outfielder, Ricky," Jesse coached as we ran to the outfield.

I misjudged the first fly ball as it soared over my head. The second fly ball, I let bounce first before picking it up and anemically throwing it back to the infield. I dropped the third and fourth balls, hit to me as the other boys chuckled at my fumbling. Jesse jabbed at those who were within reach and laughing too rigorously at me. And as his turns came up, he caught every ball with an enthusiasm and mimetic professionalism that made the other boys and coaches swoon with envy and delight.

"Okay, guys," one of the coaches barked, "thanks for showing up. The results will be in Thursday's paper, so look for your name to see what team you're on. Show up for practice on Saturday. All teams will meet here first. The season starts in one month."

"Well," I announced calmly to my mother on Thursday, feeling a sense of relief, "I didn't make it in Little League. Now what do you want me to do?"

My mother, who was washing some dishes, grabbed the newspaper from me, and with rabid and foamy hands started furiously separating the pages, not really knowing what she was looking for and not really looking. "*Cómo que,* you didn't make it? All my boys play Little League," she said as she frowned at pages she could not read.

"Well, I'm not like your other boys," I meekly explained. "I didn't grow up with them, or with anybody."

My mother put the paper down and stared at me. "What do you mean?" she said as the expression on her face shifted from a frown to one of confusion. Then she explained, "You have had a very good upbringing compared to your brothers and sisters." And then she snapped, "Now look for your name!"

"I already did," I said. "There is one Coronado, and his name is Fred."

"Well, maybe they make a mistake," she said with growing irritation. "Call the paper and see what they say."

"I'm not going to call the paper," I protested. "There is another Coronado family in this town. They have boys, too."

"I don't care about no other Coronados," she bit back. "You call and make sure!"

The lady at the newspaper was helpful enough. She gave me the phone number of the coach who had drafted this Fred Coronado, who was unknowingly making my life more miserable.

"Hello, Coach García?" I started. "Is Fred Coronado a mistake? My name is Ricky Coronado and I am calling to see if Fred is supposed to be Ricky."

"Are you related to Bernardo?" he asked.

"No. I am related to Hilario, Roberto, Andrés, and Ignacio," I said with pride as I called out my older brothers' names. "But they didn't move here with us."

"Well, no son, I know Fred because his older brother Bernardo is already on my team. Check the rest of the teams carefully. You might be on one of those."

"Okay, I called everybody," I reported to my mom, who was still washing dishes. "Nobody picked me. Now can I do what I want to do for the summer?"

"All you want to do for the summer is stay in your room and read like a *huevon* and play with the dog," she pestered. "How come you don't go do what the other boys do?"

"Because I tried to do what the other boys do and I'm not good enough! Okay?" The emotion tightened my chest as I was about to explode with frustration and humiliation.

She refused to hear me and continued as she shuffled plates into the dish rack. "Look at Eddie Brown and Jesse Colmenares. They like to do lots of things. Why can't you be like those boys?"

The fuse had finally burned down to ignite a cache of collective feelings and confused memories. "Because they have real fathers!" I exploded. "And everybody in their family is the same age. They stick together!"

I didn't know my mother could move like that. She seemed to gracefully turn from the kitchen sink and glide towards me in one athletic movement as she deftly dismissed a plate into one of the slots of the dish rack. The blow caught the side of my face with an open-handed announcement that left me stunned.

"If I ever hear you say anything like that again, *muchachito*, I will take you outside so you can feel what it is like to be beat with a *manguera*," she warned. "And that hose hurts more than a belt!"

I didn't cry for too long as I enjoyed the solitude of my room. I looked at the cover of the library book and checked the due date before pondering the title. "Hmmm, *Fear Strikes Out*," I said to myself. "This sounds like a good one."

The first time I felt it, I was at the back of the bus. I had the whole back seat to myself as Father López drove us from our public school to Saint Joseph's church. I liked Father López because he could answer all of my innocent questions. He was the one who explained to me that puppies go to heaven, too, when he found out I was distraught over my puppy being killed when my mother unknowingly ran over it in the garage.

We were going to catechism, which usually put a damper on our day when we had to attend on Saturdays. But when we went to catechism during the week, and we got out of school a couple of hours early for this, it was more fun because we felt, as fifth graders, that we were getting out of something. Even though we would soon be paying attention to a more serious and stern instructor, Sister Josephine.

We filed onto the bus. I had obnoxiously and brazenly made sure I was the first one on so I could claim the whole back seat without having to share with anybody. There were only about a dozen of us who made this weekly pilgrimage, so seats or sections of seats became personal territory as we enjoyed the short ride across town.

I had had a good day thus far, and I wasn't about to let catechism interfere with the memories of my stellar perfor- mance on the football field during recess. The fourth graders were really impressed, especially Terri Holt, the apple of my prepubescent eye. And I felt good about this.

The old school bus rattled through town as the electricity of excited children reached a squirming and swollen pitch. Boys and girls teased one another about who liked who. A few little girls sat together and talked about personal things as they held each other's hands. Jesse Colmenares studied the streets to see if any of his older brothers were cutting school. Alberto Balderas read his catechism book—Sister Josephine terrified him, so he tried harder than the rest of us. We enjoyed our own little worlds.

As I restlessly bounced up and down on the back seat, I relived the dramatic run I had made earlier that day. I had knocked Keith Wilson down on my way to pay dirt, and this was quite a feat as he was the biggest fifth grader. I rapidly drummed my fists on the seat as I made myself bounce more. I stretched out like a resting father in a hammock and looked at the dull yellow ceiling of the bus. I shifted and turned as I assumed a prostrate position. And that is when I first felt it.

As I beat the seat rapidly with my fists, I tensed my pelvic muscles and slowly ground my hips deeper into the seat. My body shivered with a tickling and tingling sensation. I slowly relaxed my hip muscles, tensed again, and pushed my quivering body into the cushion. I could feel myself pulsating and growing hard. My drumming fists had relented and were now clutching the end of the seat. I drove my hips into the sensuous padding as I lightly moaned from the current that tantalizingly shocked my body. There was a piercing cry from the school bus as it pulled into the church parking lot with screaming brakes.

I sat up quickly and looked ahead as classmates began to shuffle off the bus. I sat stunned for what seemed like minutes until I discovered I was on the bus alone. I held onto the seats in front of me and on either side of the aisle as I slowly pulled myself up, while I confusingly looked down at the area between my legs. I walked to the front of the bus and stepped down into the parking lot where Sister Josephine and her wooden ruler were waiting.

"Come on, Ricky Coronado," she warned, "Are you starting to goof off already?"

"Hello, Sister Josephine." I lightly smiled into her serious eyes. "May I get a drink of water before we go in?"

"I got you a job!" she announced as she pushed through the front door holding bags of groceries in her arms. I was reclining on the living room floor with my hands clasped, cradling the back of my head which was comfortably supported by a pillow. My attention was still focused on the action from the television as my mother headed into the kitchen.

I casually replied, "I'm not looking for a job. I'm only ten-years old."

"Don't get smart with me, boy," she shot back as she plopped her load on the table. "You'll be working all day this Saturday. And Sunday after church if you're not finished by Saturday."

My interest was dissipating from the drama on the television as Moe was about to poke his fingers into Curly's eyes and yank a clump of Larry's hair out of his head. "Ohhh, a wise guy, eh?" Curly shrieked as Larry let out a painful "yyyyaaaaahhhh!" "Okay, now spread out, you muttonheads. We gotta find that tomb of King Ruten Tuten," Moe ordered. His harsh, bossy voice was overwhelmed by my mother's explanation of the impending job duties.

I sat up and painfully listened as my mother began to put the groceries away. "You're going to work for Paul; he owns the P Market. He has five acres, and he wants somebody to pull the weeds. You know the land across the street from the graveyards? Well, you're going to work there."

"Why are there two cemeteries here anyway?" I asked, shifting the subject. "This town isn't even that big."

"Never mind about that!" she ordered. "You get to let one of your friends help you, and it won't be that Eddie Brown. He's too *travieso*. And not Jesús Colmenares either; he just likes to play baseball. Alberto Balderas is going with you.

He's a good worker. I already talk to his mother, and she says he will be there."

"How much do we get paid?" I asked, contemplating whether I wanted to do this and knowing I had no choice.

"You? Hah!" she snorted. "I already pay you with room and board and the clothes you wear, and you get everything you want already."

"I'll bet Albert will get to keep his money," I chided.

"I don't care about that!" she yelled as she continued to busily put groceries away.

I began to think of the working conditions I might experience. "It's going to be hot out there, and it might be a sin to make a kid work like that. I have to look it up."

"Don't get smart with me, Ricardito. Beside, it's too late. Paul already give me a check for twenty dollars, and that's that," she said as she ended her part of the labor negotiations.

"Twenty dollars?" I asked, shocked at the exploitation. "It will take us all day to clean that place."

"Then work fast," she indifferently suggested. And then pleading, "And do a good job. Please, don't embarrass me. I told him you're a good worker because I'm a good worker."

"Then why don't you do it?" I asked in all earnestness.

"*No me provoques, hombrecito*, okay?" she warned.

"I'm not provoking you. I barely know what that word means." My desperation grew creative. "We're not supposed to work on Sundays," I implored with righteousness and attempted to continue, "and if we don't—"

"Then finish on Saturday," she interrupted. "That way you rest on Sunday."

At this point, my mother exited the kitchen to complete her final verbal assault. "You're going to get a social security card, too, because this year you'll learn the meaning of hard work and *responsabilidad*. When you finish that job, I have another one for you. You and Mónica and me will go to pick grapes this year. Last year we got here too late."

I returned to my source of entertainment to see Moe, Larry, and Curly running away from a stiff and slowly pursuing mummy as the squeaky theme song indicated the end of another exciting episode. As I dejectedly retreated to my room, I dreamed about having my own private, peaceful place, just like King Ruten Tuten.

"Okay, *ya, levántate*, get up. We gotta go," my mother said as she shook the peaceful sleep from me.

"Is Mónica up yet?" I asked with comparative concern.

"Don't worry about it," she said gruffly. "We have to leave by 5:30 because it takes about thirty minutes to get there."

"How come Ramón doesn't have to go?" I asked as we pulled out of the driveway and into the dark world.

"Because he already retired," she said with impatience. "Remember what I told you last night."

"Yes, remember what she told you last night," Mónica echoed from the front seat. There was a taunting officiousness to her tone, and as I sat in the back seat of the car, I wanted to pounce on her for being so awake and happy at such a ridiculous hour.

"Shut up, Mónica," I said.

"Don't talk to your sister that way!" my mom ordered as we drove along black roads with vineyards on either side of them. She then began to quiz me about the coaching she had provided the night before.

"What did I tell you?" my mother demanded.

"Well, you told me a lot of things," I began, "like wash my hands after I touch the dog. And quit smelling my fingers after I scratch myself. And—"

"I mean about last night!" she fired back.

"You really should do something about his mouth, mother," my sister suggested. "He is such a smart aleck."

"I'm too tired to do anything," my mother lamented. "I raise all you kids, and for eight years I don't have no babies; then he cames along." Then she aimed her words at me. "But, yes, don't get smart-alex with me, specially when we're working with all those people. Do you understand?"

"Yes, 'um," I answered with the respect of an indentured servant.

"You see, he's doing it again!" Mónica pointed out to my mother. "I don't believe him!" And she shook her head negatively.

I sat in the back seat of the car as daylight emerged with the promise of another hot day. I thought about everything my mom had instructed me on in preparation for my maiden run at picking grapes. "When we are out there," she said, "I want you to keep working, keep picking. They don't pay us by the hour, so you have to move *con ánimo*. If you keep working, the three of us can make some good money; they pay seven cents a tray. And when we eat lunch, we only rest for thirty minutes and don't eat a lot. If you rest too long or eat too much, you become too *huevon* and then you're not good for *nada*. Don't goof off and don't worry about what the others do. Just work and mind your own business. This only will last for about six weeks, so we got to make what we can."

The veteran proletarian pulled her car off to the side of the road and in behind another car. Eager people got out of lethargic vehicles and quickly strode to the waiting vineyards. The early morning air was crisp, but the rising sun proclaimed that this would soon change.

"Okay, *vámonos*," my mother urged as she put the car in park, made the sign of the cross, and opened her door. "And remember what I told you."

"Yes, remember what she told you," Mónica recited, chuckling as she slammed the car door.

"I know," I muttered to myself as they went to the trunk of the car to get the knives and buckets. "Don't stick things in my ears and nose."

There were only two more weeks to go. My mother had been right—the harvest would last about six weeks. The seven cents a tray we earned picking grapes and sacrificing them to the sun to be turned into raisins seemed like very little compared to our ravenous efforts.

I had held up rather well so far, but mainly through the forceful encouragement of my mother who had a way of presenting a bleak future should I decide not to conform to her law. The three of us—my mom, my sister Mónica, and I—had become proud of our ability to withstand six sun-soaked days a week in the baked San Joaquin valley vineyards.

It was during the third week of our blind ambition that my mother informed us that she would no longer be accompanying and supervising our efforts. "I got that job at the rest home," my mother explained, "so you two keep working till the picking's over, and Ramón can still work in the house. I'll be working nights."

"Why do we have to keep working?" I asked. "You'll be making more than both of us."

"You only have three weeks more to go," she ordered, "and then you get to start school."

"I don't *get* to start school, I *have* to start school," I pointed out with emphasis on key words.

"Yes, that's true, *hijito,* and you don't *get* to go to work, you *have* to go to work," she teased. And she and Mónica looked at each other and laughed.

Worry consumed Mónica's face as she considered more profoundly the announcement our mother had delivered. "You mean I have to work alone with *him*?" Mónica asked incredulously. I smiled a bashful and innocent radiance as I looked at my judges. "He is not going to mind me, Mom," Mónica said with assurance.

"I don't have to mind anybody!" I replied. "I work hard."

"See, he's starting already. I know what he's going to be like when you're not there," she prognosticated.

"Oh, don't worry about that," my mom said with a sinister tone to her voice. "He will mind everything you tell him, or he will know what it's like to eat and sleep with the dog!"

Mónica looked at me. Her pursed lips and raised eyebrows suggested victory.

We had gotten along surprisingly well without our mother. Our pace was a serious one. At the end of each work day, we felt great satisfaction and pride at having put forth such a sincere effort. Without the furious urgency of our mother, our lunchtime menu had become more creative. We froze cans of soda pop the night before each work day and wrapped them in aluminum foil so they would still be cold enough when we took our break. We were still only allotted one burrito each for lunch, and whatever grapes we wanted to eat. We also learned to bring our own toilet paper for the ill-equipped and flimsy cubicle that represented an outhouse.

I'm not sure what happened the morning I went on strike. I remember feeling a profound loneliness and sadness that overtook my heart and mind with an enormous sense of futility. Mónica parked the car, enthusiastically jumping out to challenge another day of labor and heat. I opened the car door slowly, but did not attempt to get out. I could feel the trunk of the car open and heard Mónica busily gathering our equipment.

"Come on, Ricky!" she urged with a voice that mimicked my mother's.

My crying was torrential from the start, and my body shook from the effect of extreme emotion. Mónica started towards the front of the car, admonishing me for my lack of movement.

"Come on, let's go, Ricky. Don't start getting lazy now. You think just because Mom—" She stopped her tongue-lashing lecture as she was shocked by my convulsing display. "What's the matter?" she asked. "What happened?" And she looked around as if to pick out a perpetrator who had committed a hurtful act upon me.

The roadside was alive with enthusiastic people. Some walked to their work eating burritos hurriedly. Others inspected their knives for sharpness.

"Ricky, what's wrong?" My sister pleaded as her face became flush with embarrassment. She knelt down at the side of the car, facing me and holding my right hand. I could not speak for many seconds.

"I, don't, want, to do this anymore," I cried. "I hate this! I'm tired. None of our friends have to work like this. Mom's just making us do this because she's mean and wants us to know what her life was like," I moaned. Then with a rising anger, "This is stupid! We're bossed around by guys who are my age. They don't even know how to work. They're just lucky their parents are rich. They'll never have to work in the dirt and hot sun with spiders running up their arms. They are a bunch of—," and the second wave of tears flooded my words so they were now just primitive groans and grunts.

"Mónica, I don't want to go out there anymore. I'm too embarrassed," I said in a pleading voice.

"Oh, Ricky," she started, "we're almost done. After this week, we're done. Come on. We can do it. We'll show Mom we can do it. School starts in a couple of weeks and then we won't have to do this anymore."

I struck back with rejuvenated anger. "I don't want to show Mom anything! She doesn't care anyway. We always have to work. And I get in trouble for doing something lazy like reading." I knew my argument made sense to my sister, mainly because it seemed so true.

"Look," she suggested, "I'll go to work and you stay in the car and rest. We'll talk about it at lunch time. Okay?"

I watched Mónica's body slowly cross the road and disappear into a row of vineyards. The guilt brought my crying to a self-pounding magnitude of grief. And for a moment, I thought of relenting to join my sister.

The light tapping on the window slowly drew me from my sleep. Mónica peered in and smiled. "I'm hungry. What's for lunch?" I offered a weak smile and unlocked the car door. We sat in the car quietly eating our lunch.

"Wow, there's still some ice in my soda," she said, attempting to strike up a meaningless conversation.

"What are you going to tell Mom?" I asked, thinking about the water hose that I had been frequently threatened with, but up to this point had never experienced. Certainly this called for water-hose-disciplinary action.

"I don't know," Mónica replied as she looked straight ahead.

"Well, I'm going back out there with you," I said. "I don't care what you tell her."

"We don't have to tell her anything," she offered.

"Yes, we do," I insisted. "Just tell her so we can get it over with."

"Look, Ricky," Mónica slowly began, "I'm sorry for all the things that we have to go through. I'm embarrassed, too, but it won't always be like this. Look at the older ones. They have good jobs and don't have to do this anymore. We will be like that, too. Really."

"I don't care," I relented. "I don't care about anything. I just wish I was dead."

"Don't say that!" she snapped. "You're young and you don't know what things will be like. You have to have faith in God. Things will get better."

After lunch, we walked back to the fields. Mónica led the way to the new parcel of land a serious young scion assigned us to work for the few days of the harvest that remained. I thought about the imminent scolding I would receive later that day and the brighter future my sister promised.

"How do you know?" I asked out loud as my thinking became vocal.

"How do I know what?"

"How do you know we are going the right way?" I answered as I revised what I really wanted to know.

I remember the announcer's statement capturing my attention like that of a dog who has been to obedience school and responds on command. I was playing with my plastic army men on the living room floor and not really paying attention to the television, whose purpose was serving more as lighting than entertainment.

"Turn that television off if you're not watching it!" my mother commanded from the kitchen.

"I am watching it," I lied as I positioned a prone army man with a rifle against one who was standing with a pistol.

I was not a football fan at the time, as I was only eleven-years old and just getting the hang of the sport. But it was on this day in 1966 that I would begin a romance with the Dallas Cowboys that would extend into my adult years. There were no Super Bowls in those days, just regular championship games.

As the laying-down soldier killed the standing army man, the announcer rousingly urged viewers to see "The Green Bay Packers led by Bart Starr and Coach Vince Lombardi as they host the Dallas Cowboys with Bob Hayes, the world's fastest human."

I let all of my army men die a quick death on the tundra of a worn carpet as I focused my attention on the announcement that had come and fleetingly gone. "Huh? What did he say about the world's fastest human?" I asked myself. I can't remember ever having been mesmerized by such a statement in all of my life.

"Hey, Mom," I yelled into the kitchen from where the sounds of cooking and the aroma of food floated, "do you know who the world's fastest human is?"

"What?" she yelled back with a tone of annoyance.

And I replied with a convenient, "Never mind," knowing questions and other interruptions often led to work, or a quick trip to the store, or some other oppressive price for imparted information.

I studied the television for some time, not concerned with the program that was on, but waiting for the advertisement to reappear. A commercial encouraged viewers to, "try new Coca-Cola—without cyclamates." Another invited smokers to enjoy a unique cigarette "with a micronite filter." I waited with the patience of a detective on a stakeout as I sat cross-legged and directly in front of the television. Finally, after hearing about the terrific weight-loss benefits of Metrecal, the excited announcer's voice repeated the remarkable claim. Again, I was entranced by the statement that spoke of the world's fastest human.

"How do they know?" I wondered out loud. "I wonder how they know he is the world's fastest human? Did they get everyone in the world to race somewhere and this guy won? Wow, the fastest human in the whole world!" And I was struck with awe.

"Close your mouth; it'll attract flies," my older brother Nacho teasingly warned as he walked into the house. "What's wrong with you?"

"Hey, Nacho," I started, "do you know who the world's fastest human is?"

"You mean Bob Hayes?" he nonchalantly asked.

"How did you know that?"

"Because those ads have been running all week," he confessed.

"How do they know Bob Hayes is the world's fastest human?" I continued.

"Because of the Olympics," he answered as he turned the channel to watch Show Time Wrestling.

"The which?" I persisted.

"The Olympics," he glibly repeated.

"What's that?"

"The Olympics happens every four years, and that's when they race and find out who the world's fastest human is," he reported.

"Wow!" I said. "They have a race every four years to see who the fastest guy in the world is! Where do these guys come from?"

"I don't know. All over, I guess," Nacho replied. I could tell by the tone of his answer that my questioning was beginning to create a degree of irritation.

"Well, did *you* race to see if you were one of the fastest humans in the world?" I asked with genuine inquisitiveness.

"No! Now leave me alone or I'll show you who the world's fastest fighter is," he warned.

As the wrestlers were introduced, a handsome one from San Francisco and a masked one from "parts unknown," I continued to wonder about the world's fastest human. He didn't seem human at all the more I thought about it. The crowd cheered as they urged the handsome wrestler to take the mask off his mysterious challenger. I went into the kitchen to assess the feeding schedule and said out loud to nobody, "I can't wait to see the world's fastest human."

My mother, who was stirring crackling meat in a frying pan, calmly said, "Who, Bob Hayes?"

The first time I saw him, there was blood all over his face. The coach said, "I think your nose is broke, David. That ball took a wicked hop. I don't think you should play today."

"I think I can handle it, coach," he replied as he attempted to wipe flowing blood from his mouth and chin. "At least let me try the first couple of innings."

David played the entire game and hit a home run and a triple. He also flawlessly fielded everything hit to him. That day he replaced Bob Hayes, the world's fastest human, as my hero. I had a vested interest in this athlete as he was my sister's boyfriend and the talk of the local baseball enthusiasts. It concerned me that the relationship was a strong one, because to know David was to know a local star.

Newspapers frequently wrote about him and featured pictures of his outstretched body parallel to the ground as he speared searing ground balls, recovered, and threw out frustrated runners at first. Other newspaper pictures captured him at the plate in the middle of his sweet, fluid swing.

He was a modest star and that's what I really liked about him. His kind blue eyes always greeted me with an attention that caused deep sighs of adulation. He was not loud and did not ever admit that he was an attraction to other young boys like myself, or to budding high school girls who envied my sister's luck.

His mannerisms were complacent. He would wave by holding up a still hand at about shoulder height for a few seconds, then return to whatever it was he was doing.

I knew this ballplayer was a special person as he had the respect of my brothers who thought Al Capone was a sissy for getting caught. It was my brothers who collectively agreed that to "deny, deny, deny" was the best way out of anything accusatory. Then use force if necessary.

David once gave me his baseball mitt. It was a Rawlings with Clete Boyer's autograph. Even though I never played on a baseball team, I once made it to the final cuts with that glove. For a short, bittersweet time, I became a better baseball player because of that talismanic glove. David spent hours with me, teaching me how to hit and field, but mostly infusing my life with a confidence that I frequently tried to deny.

Of course, my sister had a headlock on the relationship. And at times I felt I was competing for something that rightfully belonged to her. Whenever David was around, my sister would attempt to shoo me away so they could be alone. But I was like a bothersome fly; I would disappear for a little while and then return to catch David's tentative hand holding my sister's hand.

One of my proudest moments was when my sister announced that she and David would be getting married. Through the residual effect of being my sister's little brother, I could flaunt that David, a future big leaguer, would be my brother-in-law. I, in turn, announced to Eddie Brown, Jesse Colmenares, and Alberto Balderas that, yes, it was true, David the star would be related to me. For weeks I walked around with a hubris that was nauseating to my friends, especially since I was never talented enough to make it on a baseball team despite five humiliating attempts.

During those days of my infatuation with baseball and my future brother-in-law, little else attracted my attention. I would scan the sports section of the local paper after every game that David played to see how he had done. When I could attend his games, I was his personal statistician. I had a little piece of paper with columns denoting at bats, hits, type of hit, runs, and runs batted in. Upon returning home, I would log the figures into the cumulative totals that I kept on a large piece of cardboard tacked to my bedroom wall. I never kept track of any errors David made. I ignored errors—which were too few anyway—and always convinced myself and any others who would listen that the ball must have taken a wicked hop.

# 13

My mother had a rather quirky way of preparing my stepfather and me for church each Sunday. Every Sabbath morning seemed to begin with her cursing us into action and scolding us for our lack of motion, along with telling us what we would be wearing to mass.

"Don't take a long shower. And wear the clothes I hang up on your closet door," my mother mandated.

"You mean the ones with *sonday* written on the paper and taped to my pants?" I asked, already knowing the curt answer.

"Yes!"

As she removed herself from yelling into the locked bathroom door to give my stepfather his orders, I said, "You spelled Sunday wrong." The doorknob was harassed as my mother attempted to break in to tell me what she thought of my comment.

"I don't care about that!" she informed. "I didn't went to school, son. I do my best. Now hurry up!"

My stepfather was next in her sights as she pointed out his attire for the day. "And wear a tie *Ramoncito*."

"*Sí, mamí,*" he respectfully submitted.

"We will go to a different church this time," she informed us as we got into the car.

"You mean we're not Catholics anymore?" I asked, knowing what she really meant, but wishing to return some of the grief she had burdened me with by making me go to church on Sunday and confession on Saturday.

She turned around to face me as I sat slumped in the back seat. "Sit up straight. And here, this is for the *limosna*," she said as she ignored my question and handed me various coins for the collection plate. "And make sure you put it all in!"

"Okay, which way, *Querida*?" my stepfather asked as my mother navigated our way to the new church.

"Keep going, I tell you where," she responded.

We filed into a pew, my mother, my stepfather, and then me. I sat on the end, which was always my favorite place to sit in church. It allowed me the opportunity to make a quick escape as mass ended. My mother was annoyed because we did not get a pew up front. Instead, we were relegated to inconspicuous back-of-the-church worship. I beamed at my fortune: sitting on the end and toward the back. I would not have to slither my way through too many people to get out, I thought. And I reviewed my exit strategy as mass was beginning.

Over the past few months, during mass, my stepfather and I had serendipitously discovered a little game in which, kneeling side by side, with our hands engaged to denote pious prayer, my right elbow would meet with his left elbow as we rested our arms on the back of the pew that was in front of us. I would apply pressure to his elbow with mine, and he would reciprocate. It was like a reverse tug-of-war. We did this every time the kneeling part came around. My mother never noticed, as we usually pushed to a standoff while she bent her head in devotion.

Maybe we weren't accustomed to the pews of this different church. Or maybe we were feeling high-spirited that glorious Sunday morning. My stepfather started the jousting and, naturally, I was prepared. He slowly and forcefully pushed against my elbow with his, and I waited for the tension to ease so I could take my turn. But my turn didn't seem to come. He kept pushing and I could feel my entire body start to give way. I imagined a dramatic situation as I mentally repeated, "Mayday! Mayday! We have heavy incoming!..."

As the pushing increased and my body began to tilt toward the aisle, I gave myself the order to "Return fire!" and began a furtive push with my elbow. I slowly regained lost territory as my leaning, kneeling posture straightened. Both our bodies grew more rigid, and finally my stepfather's strength started to take a nose dive. I relished my new position as the priest continued the ritual in which my stepfather and I participated in physical presence only.

I pushed even harder as my youthful strength started my stepfather's body to tilt towards my mother's. "Victory!" I thought to myself, and kept pushing until my stepfather was destroyed. His body tumbled into my mother's, whose body was jolted sideways, disrupting the devotee kneeling next to her.

It was difficult to contain my laughter, but I succeeded by burying my face in my prayerful hands. My stepfather knelt upright and attempted to help my mother who was apologizing to the upset parishioner. Her look told my stepfather there would be a serious conference later as she disgustingly but subtly pushed him away. I maintained my posture of supplication. I could sense my mother craning her neck to look past my stepfather and fire the same look at me. I did not return eye contact. I furrowed my brow in extreme unction and prayerfully pleaded for forgiveness.

"The mass is ended. Go in peace," said Father somebody. As the respondents replied a robot-like "Thanks be to God," I spewed a hasty "Thanks God" and bolted from my advantageous position. I admired myself for being one of the first ones out. A couple of other boys had beat me to it, but I assured myself that they knew this church and I was in foreign territory.

I leaned against the car as I waited for my mother and stepfather. My mother exchanged pleasant nods and goodbyes with others. As she approached the car, her visage promised trouble.

"Get in the car," she ordered, and then flashed a holy smile to a passing church member.

The parking lot was emptying, but my mother did not allow my stepfather to start the car. "What do you think you was doing?" my mother demanded as she looked at my stepfather and then turned to look at me. "I don't believe you *condenados* act that way in the house of the Lord!" she began. "You should be ashamed of yourself, Ramón del Sol. And you, *jodón*," as she directed her barrage at me, "you will see what happens when we get home."

"I sorry, hoooneyyyy," my stepfather replied as he tried to suppress his laughter.

"Yeah, I'm sorry, too, Mom," I said with semi-sincerity, knowing she could still inflict pain upon me.

"No, I'm sorry nor nothing," she answered. "You two have embarrassed me in front of everyone." And then she hit us with a most bizarre proclamation: "*Ya, no más.* That's it. You two are not going to church with me again! *¡Nunca!* From now on, I go by myself."

My stepfather shifted in his seat a little and tried to look at me through the rearview mirror. What my mother perceived as hurtful news came as a joyous revelation to both of us. Oh, I knew that the rest of that day I would be banished to a life of hard labor, probably pulling weeds or cleaning the kitchen, or both. But it no longer mattered if my Sundays were to be released from the bondage of forced religion. My mind raced at the combinations of possibilities that destiny could grant me. "If I don't have to go to church on Sundays," I thought, "that also means I don't have to go to confession on Saturdays. And that means that Albert Balderas, Jesse Colmenares, and Eddie Brown won't make fun of me when I ride my bike to church all dressed up."

She continued in a threatening tone, "You think life is a game. *Bueno,* I got other games you two can play. Now that you're not going to church with me—"

My stepfather could not take it any longer as he interrupted, "*¡Oh no, mami! Por favor,* please, let us to go to church with you, please." And he pleaded for mercy with the sincerity of a bogus, bad-guy wrestler who feigns imminent defeat.

"Yeah, Mom, please, please, please let us to go to church with you," I mockingly wailed. "We can't stay at home alone on Sundays."

My mother grew silent and stared at each of us with her green tiger-like eyes. And then, shifting her locked gaze straight ahead at nothing, she calmly delivered the final blow as she held her rosary and prayer book. "Oh, you are not gonna be alone at home on Sundays. Because you will go to the eight o'clock mass from now on. I will still go to the 11 o'clock mass, and the both of you two will be working until I get home! And remember, I like to go to the graveyard, Long's, and the *panadería* after church." She ordered my stepfather to start the car and take us home.

As we pulled out of the parking lot, I said to myself, "The mass is ended. Go in peace."

# 14

When we did it, it was always in the garage. It had to be that way because my mother wouldn't let us make *menudo* in her kitchen; she said it created a smell that would linger for days.

It's true, there is a bit of an olfactory hit from the boiling of the tripe. But knowing how savory the finished product would be was always worth the effort.

My stepfather, a jack-of-all-trades, built a table especially suited for us to work at comfortably while accommodating all of our equipment and materials. The table was rectangular in shape and about the height of a conventional kitchen table. The top was regular plywood with legs cut from two-by-fours. Situated in the middle but placed more toward the back of the table top, was a crude cast iron two-burner stove. From the back of the stove ran a hose for each burner; the other ends of the hoses were attached to two chubby butane cylinders placed directly under the table and out of the way.

My stepfather was methodical in his approach—in anything he did—and only those willing to serve as apprentices were invited to work with him. I deemed it an honor when he chose me to help him in the lengthy process of cooking *menudo*. My mother claims that my stepfather had no choice but to ask me to help him as I was the one who devoured most of the red spicy soup. My sister Mónica, knowing my stepfather's meticulous peculiarities, was surprised that I was so willing. "I must learn the ways of my people," I joked.

I felt like an acolyte assisting his patron the first time my stepfather explained the process to me.

The table had enough space on each end for us to do the cutting and chopping of ingredients, while at the same time keeping the ingredients directly in front of us within convenient reach. We sat on old chairs that my mother had tried to throw away, but were saved by the handy work of my stepfa-

ther. We used a large blue pot with white speckles, and only
menudo could be cooked in this. It was a house rule. We filled
the menudo pot with water and placed it on the rustic stove;
the pot was situated in such a way that it consumed most of
the two burners. Lazy blue flames from each burner tickled
opposite sides of the large vessel, while more active flames
blazed underneath it.

My stepfather salted the water. He carefully unwrapped
the *patas* and cut the hoofs in half, placing them in the heat-
ing water. I washed the tripe in the utility sink, then cleaned
it by scraping away the fat and trimming any unsightly blem-
ishes. We worked with sharp knives as each of us took sheets
of tripe and cut it into little squares.

As the water heated, my stepfather prepared the table for
the next step. We would be blending California and *ancho*
chilies after cleaning them of stems and seeds. We would also
be adding onion, garlic, black pepper, and eventually hominy.
But all of this was to occur over lengthy intervals of time. The
water and the cow's hoofs and the pieces of stomach lining
would have to simmer for a couple of hours before we added
the rest of the ingredients. During that time, my stepfather
and I would take turns attending to the seething pot. We
checked the heat and skimmed the top of the mixture of
excess fragments.

We only made menudo during the winter holidays. My
stepfather was proud of his cooking method. He liked to start
the project in the afternoon, carefully tending to the broth
throughout the night, and joyfully serving it for breakfast the
following morning. During the first interval of time, we would
eat dinner. We played cards or watched television for the
remaining intervals we were awake, while the menudo
chugged away in the garage. During the late night and early
morning hours of the process, my stepfather was the watcher
of the pot. He would stir the concoction, add other ingredients
like hominy, and stoop and squint at the flames as they
worked under the cauldron.

The following morning, as the menudo reached its point
of epicurean greatness, we were allowed to complete the final
stage in my mother's kitchen. I prepared the garnishes: lemon
wedges, chopped onion, dried oregano, and crushed *japonés
chile*. My mother heated the *comal* to warm the corn tortillas.
And my stepfather shuffled back and forth between the

kitchen and garage to insure that final phases of the event were going according to plan. He would rub his hands and gleefully sway from side to side, as if he were dancing a *corrido*, and then he checked the steaming pot of the red and chunky soup. "*Ya merito, ya merito,*" he would announce, letting us know it was almost ready, as he turned the flames down.

As we sat to eat, my stepfather would take a large bowl and go to the garage for the first helping. He entered the kitchen, and with great flourish, he held in front of him a steaming bowl of thick soup with half-a-hoof conspicuously placed in the middle. This was for my mother, who loved the *pata*. The next bowl was usually for me, and it contained an abundance of hominy, which was to my particular liking.

As my stepfather placed his bowl on the table, he would make the sign of the cross and give thanks to God before sitting down. Being more of a pagan myself, I usually had already begun eating by the time my mother and stepfather joined me. It was then that I would make a hasty attempt at crossing myself. My mother would lightly curse me, and my stepfather would laugh as we enjoyed the lively, pungent soup.

## 15

The instruments of their butchery were savagely sharp. They used crude knives with simple wooden handles. A hacksaw, its blade layered with dried blood from previous killings, was used for those parts protected by thick bone that were hard to cut.

Many times as I approached my yard after school, I could sense the death, and see the fragments of the slaughtered innocent animals sacrificed to feed the guilty. There were goat skulls lying in the yard—the jaw bones had been ripped away from their flesh-picked heads to be used as toy guns. That was last night's meal—goat's head soup. The remaining body parts of the goat: ribs, neck, and shanks were being slowly cooked in the backyard pit as we anticipated *una pajanga de birria.*

A few days later I could tell there were fresh and bloody rabbit pelts in the garbage barrel as a squadron of flies hovered busily over the barrel, and many more made unrelenting sorties into the cylinder of skins. The meaty remnants of rabbit were cooked with tomatoes and chiles. Occasionally, an unlucky pig would be conscripted from a neighbor's small farm. Its main offering of *carnitas* was enjoyed for days.

I was grateful that my mother and stepfather did not require me to stay and help with the swift and skilled throat-slitting of the pigs or goats and the head-knocking of the rabbits as they teamed to mug our next meal. I did not like the squealing, screaming, shocked sounds of death, and I made it a point to remain coolly impersonal with these victims while they lived in my presence. My affection was granted only to the dog. I was sure she would still be alive when I returned from my solo sojourns in the vineyards. So I was allowed to leave during the time it took to prepare the animal for cooking, often returning to ironic smells that teased my nose and taste buds.

On other days, I would open the oven door slowly to find a fully displayed cow's tongue—*lengua*—silently mocking its own death and daring me to eat it. One day, my mother sliced the tongue and put it in the refrigerator. My brother-in-law, a *gabacho*, made a beautiful sandwich with white bread, lettuce, mayonnaise, tomato, and slabs of the sliced tongue. My mother and sister came home from work to find him sitting comfortably in the living room, watching a baseball game and devouring his sandwich.

"What are you eating?" asked my sister curiously.

"A roast beef sandwich," mumbled my brother-in-law, as he tried to answer with a glutted mouth. "It's good!"

My mother chuckled as she went to her bedroom saying something about a *"pobre gabachito,* when will he learn?"

"That's not roast beef, you nut," my sister scoffed in a wifely manner, knowing her husband would be surprised at the anatomical information she was about to deliver. "It's tongue!"

My brother-in-law's face turned an ash-pale as he stopped his vigorous chewing. He rose slowly and sickly as my mother was now putting her apron on and warning him not to throw the sandwich away. "Give your roast beef sandwich to Ricky or the dog." A tradition was started as my mother frequently teased my brother-in-law by inviting him to a flavorful dinner of *"lengua de* roast beef."

Our kitchen often contained many surprises. Sometimes the oven would yield a flat pan of cooked intestines lying in a serpentine squiggle. Or there would be the *menudo* with its cut squares of stomach lining and cow's hoofs simmering on a burner. Occasionally, goats' heads could be found bobbing in a large pot of water, their mouths opened as if they were screaming silently from a watery hell.

Animals did not fare well with us. We spared the dog and often warned her that she should consider herself one of God's lucky ones.

## 16

There was a group of us, and we all had a name for each other besides the ones our parents lovingly and thoughtfully christened us with. It was funny how we named each other. Some of us were nicknamed what we were because of activities we participated in. I was Ricky Rabbit or *Conejo* because my stepfather and I raised rabbits—many rabbits—to sell to our modest clientele. Another contributing factor was that my family lived in a small San Joaquin valley community known as Conejo while all of my other friends were officially residents of contiguous Selma.

Some of my friends were nicknamed because of their appearance. Gilbert Reyna was Moose because he was gangly and awkward. His extremely bucked teeth, uncombed curly hair, and thickly-lensed glasses inspired someone to amend his name to Professor Moose. Gregorio Olivas was *Mole* because of his dark complexion. Albert Balderas was Chopper because he was missing a couple of fingers due to a lesson gone awry on how to butcher a goat. Vicente Zavala's other name was Stitch because he had a viciously ugly scar that ran from under his chin and off into the direction of an ear. "A doctor slipped when he was operating on me," was Stitch's reason for being who he was. Eddie Brown was Big Ears. But our community was pretty bilingual, so he was also *Orejón*. It all made sense to us one day when someone got studious and said that they had read that Oregon was called Oregon because it was the land of big-eared men. It was such a remarkable revelation when we put two and two together and discovered that Eddie Brown had been born in Eugene!

The way someone else's real names sounded determined his nickname. For instance, Javier Noriega was *Borrega* or Lamb because his last name resembled the Spanish word for lamb. When we really wanted to remind him of his nickname, we called him Girlie Lamb; it was more accurate.

And then there was Tadeo. None of us had ever heard of such a first name. We thought and thought one day trying to figure out if any one of us had a relative or friend by that name.

"Where did you get that name anyway?" we wondered.

"From the Bible," was his humble answer. And we respected that, kind of. But we couldn't stand just calling him plain Tadeo. As an experiment, we started out by attaching the prefix "Po" which gave us PoTadeo. We pronounced it in English again and again until it came to sound like "potato." So Tadeo became Potato or *Patata*.

Those of us who knew Valentín Camacho referred to him as *Vale,* which is also a form of the Spanish word *valor,* or value. So we attached "no" to his shortened version and came up with *No Vale.*"

It seemed to me that a lot of creativity had been expended to come up with our social names. But the way they worked was a bit perverse. Our names were used to vilify each other. And none of us liked, or was supposed to like, our nicknames. Whenever disputes arose like the one Eddie Brown started one day when he tried to tell all of us that the English word for passing gas was *fart* and not *fark* as the rest of us knew the phenomenon to be, we collectively maligned him and his corrections with many epithets of Big Ears and *Orejón.*

Other times our rhetoric was much more subtle. A favorite method of insult was to allude to our nicknames by incorporating them in the recounting of an alleged television program. For instance, when Vicente tried to tell us that he had seen a program about "A rabbit with big big ears, I mean real *orejas,*" and that the owner of this pet was feeding him potatoes and *mole,* and that the rabbit's best friends were an ugly moose with chopped off antlers that wasn't worth anything and a little girlie lamb with a chopped off tail that was even worth less, it did not take much imagination for the rest of us to figure out we had all been slandered.

"Oh, yeah?" Javier asked with a tone of bitter revenge, "And did the rabbit have a big *STITCH* running from under his chin to his big ears?"

And now Eddie Brown, realizing the added offense, attacked Javier with "Hey! Did I call you a name, Girlie Lamb?"

And as the rest of us attempted to get even with Stitch and each other, a free-for-all of slander ensued.

It was important not to let our family know about these names because we all had brothers and sisters who could use them against us. My older brother Nacho, unbeknown to me, once got a hold of my P.E. t-shirt that my mother had just washed, and in tiny letters on the back wrote "Ricky Rabbit is a fat rabbit." I did not discover this until we were drawing up sides to play soccer in P.E., and Valentín read out loud, with grandiloquence, the back of my shirt: "RICKY RABBIT, IS, A, FAT RABBIT. I didn't know that," he commented with purported seriousness, "but that's what it says on the back of your shirt."

The class applauded and roared, and I was left with a weak retort that nobody heard: "*Pues, no vale* then, huh?"

It wasn't until I moved away that I lost my nickname. I never revealed to my new group of friends that I had been known as Rabbit or *Conejo*. And they just didn't have the imagination that my other friends had. I think I would've mentioned something if I had been known as Jake or Rocky or Gus or some other rugged sounding name.

# 17

My stepfather was an incredibly creative person. He had a mind that could analyze and imagine many possibilities, and then use the immediate materials available to him to fix or invent without having to spend what little money he had. He collected his materials from the dump, and he reused things like nails and wood. One of my regular chores was to sit in the backyard with a hammer and straighten out nails that were taken out of boards that my stepfather and I retrieved from condemned homes or the junk pile behind the woodshop at the high school.

To take our own trash to the dump, my stepfather built a trailer out of plywood. The rusted frame and axle of the trailer was pulled from the dump and we spent hours sandpapering the rust from it. We got the tires for the trailer from a decrepit motorcycle that looked like something from an old Marlon Brando movie. They didn't quite match, but we used them anyway. The axle hubs were exposed, which, my stepfather pointed out, would leave them at the mercy of the elements. *"Necesitamos tapones,"* he said as he scratched his head wondering.

Bent over and sifting through one of our garbage barrels, he emerged with two tomato cans, proclaiming that we now had hubcaps for our new trailer. With wire, nails, and ingenuity, he covered the hubs with the tomato cans. "Ramón del Sol not so stupid," he said as he stepped back and admired his work.

In one day we built a greenhouse in our backyard made of two-by-fours for the frame. We used various colors of plastic sheeting that we had been collecting for the sides and roof. We fastened the plastic to the frame with slats we procured from the lattice of a decaying and deserted home. It was a handsome greenhouse, but it lacked a door. He traveled to that place within his mind that created doors out of whatever

might be available, whatever their original purpose might
have been.

From our metal scrap heap he tugged at an old iron army
bed frame. He cut off the short legs of the bed and attached
door hinges to one side of it. To keep the door closed, he simply twisted some wire to the bed-frame-turned-door and
wrapped the other end around a nail that was partially ham-
mered into the door jamb. The springs in the bed frame protected the newly planted seeds inside the greenhouse from
any animal interlopers while allowing fresh air to circulate
within. My stepfather fastened a roll of plastic to the top of
the door that could be pulled down as a protective cover for
exceptionally cold nights. As he swung the door to and fro to
test its reliability, he radiated satisfaction at the completion
of yet another project.

When the heavy valley fog and the wintry rains made it
difficult for us to dry our washed clothes outside, my stepfather began to reflect on the problem. This time the wood pile
yielded the solution. He dusted off the wooden vertical bars of
a playpen historically used for incarcerating babies, making
them prisoners in their own homes. He fastened two ends of
the sides of the playpen together with door hinges and turned
the V-shaped creation upside down. After studying the now
horizontal rungs, he shook the structure lightly to test its
sturdiness. Satisfied, he placed his new invention in front of
the wall heater and draped wet clothes on the rungs. "*Vamos
a ver*," he speculated as he went on to busy himself with
another contrivance. We monitored the drying clothes and
rotated the newly-created rack as needed. It worked beautifully. With the two remaining sides of the playpen, my stepfather made another drying rack as a gift to my sister and her
family of six kids. It was a popular item.

My stepfather's creativity also helped in scholarly pur-
suits. At school, for an art and music class, I was assigned a
creative project that was to be either in art or musical form.
As I could only draw stick figures, I decided to try something
musical. It was suggested to the class by our teacher that we
could make an instrument if we felt especially creative.
Although I had no idea of what kind of instrument I wanted
to make or how to go about it, I was attracted to this
approach. I presented my dilemma to my stepfather who
promised to get back to me; he needed time to think about it.

A few days later, my stepfather summoned me to the garage which served as his workshop. After clarifying what the assignment asked me to do, he began to create. He took a two-by-four and sawed off two pieces about six inches in length. He then took two sheets of coarse sandpaper already tailored to fit the sawed pieces and instructed me to wrap them around the two blocks of wood, nailing the sandpaper to what would serve as the top of this instrument. He slid the two sandpaper-covered blocks against each other and shuffled his feet a little to indicate that we had something musical. He smiled and asked, "What do you think?"

"Okay, I guess," I answered. I told him it seemed a little awkward, that something was missing.

"*Por supuesto*," he responded assuredly, and instructed me to pay attention. From his workbench, he took two used cabinet handles made out of cheap metal. One was silver and the other was bronze in color. He screwed the cabinet handles into the top of the sanding blocks and, holding the blocks by the newly attached handles, shuffled his feet once again, rhythmically dancing to the sounds of his own creation.

I got an "A" for the sandpaper blocks.

## 18

We had been to the county fair before. But this year would be different. We were teenagers, both Eddie Brown and myself. I told my mom that we wanted to go off by ourselves and we would meet her and my stepfather later for dinner.

My mother looked at Eddie Brown suspiciously and warned, "Eddie Brown, don't get my boy in trouble." She kissed me on the cheek, and moments later we were rushing the midway.

We made it our goal to spend every last cent we had in the process of enjoying the spinning and whirling rides. As night began to fall, we staggered off a ride that had made us feel like astronauts.

"Where were we supposed to meet your parents, Ricky?" Eddie asked.

"Over by the arts and crafts building. I think they want to eat at the Mexican Village," I answered.

We walked towards the arts and crafts building while we debated which rides would cause instant death if someone were to be flung from them.

As we approached the building, we decided to rest on some picnic tables situated on a grassy knoll and under a few shade trees. From our vantage point we could scan the arts and crafts building.

"The first one to spot them, wins," Eddie declared.

"Wins what? We don't have anything," I reminded.

"Uh, let's see," Eddie Brown mused. "What could the prize be?"

"Okay," I suggested. "If I see them first, I get your Hank Aaron Louisville Slugger. If you win, you get my Western Auto bicycle frame." We shook on the deal and spied like hungry eagles.

The dull thump on the back of my head was slow to register in my mind. I looked to my left, at Eddie, to offer a punch back. He was looking past me, and as I turned, I was greeted with a stinging slap to the cheek.

"Give me all your money," the strange boy ordered. He had on black pants and black pointy shoes. His shirt was of thick cotton with long sleeves. Only the top few buttons were fastened. Underneath he wore a plain white t-shirt. His hair was gallantly slicked back and his countenance advertised terror. Behind this forceful personality stood a duplicate.

I immediately started crying and told the young men that I had no money. "I might have a quarter," I said brokenly. I reached into my pocket hoping to find currency.

The duplicate was now slapping Eddie Brown who truly had no money and was telling his broker such. We stood in the shadows of the fair. Only yards away, through blurry eyes, I could see happy people enjoying themselves. I could hear tired children asking their parents to hold them. And I could smell the various foods that permeate fairs with a delectable diversity. My mouth was dry as I discovered silver and handed a quarter to the bullying boy.

He slapped the quarter out of my hand and demanded, "Pick it up and give it to me again."

I bent over to pick up the quarter. As I started to straighten, the assailant struck me on the side of the head with his knee.

"What's the matter, fatboy," he jeered. "You don't like something?" I did not answer him, thinking the question rhetorical and also thinking it looked more respectful if I just cried and did not talk back.

"Answer me!" he said as he slapped my other cheek. The duplicate had discovered no gold with Eddie and was now laughing at me.

"I, I don't—," I weepily tried.

But the manboy slapped me again and said, "Shut up, before I really hurt you!"

They laughed as they evaporated into the darkness from where they had come. I looked over at Eddie, who had his hands in his pockets and was looking down at the ground. Without looking at me, he asked if I was okay.

"Yeah, I guess so," I replied. "How come you didn't cry Eddie?" I asked as I wiped tears from my face. "Weren't you afraid?"

"Yeah," he answered. "I was really scared, but I thought if I started crying, they would just get rougher with me like they did with you."

We did not tell my parents what happened. That night, Eddie Brown became a different person in my eyes. Up to that point we had been best friends, equals. But now, he seemed like a more mature person who could handle tense situations. I had much more respect for Eddie Brown after that day. I even considered not being his friend anymore. I didn't feel worthy.

The next day, as I sat in my bedroom reading, Eddie came over. "Hey, Ricky," he yelled as he walked down the hallway to my room, "here's that baseball bat I owe you."

# 19

I could not believe my eyes. I looked closely and attempted to shake the confusion from my mind. But my eyes relayed the same bizarre picture to me that had stirred my initial shock. They were stuck together. I mean really stuck together. It was Eddie Brown's little mutt, Blackie, and my wienie dog, Mickey. I had never seen such a sight in all of my thirteen years of living.

"Mom!" I yelled as I ran into the house screaming. "Mickey and Blackie are stuck together. I think they're hurt."

My mother dropped what she was doing and ran outside. With the movement of a devoted fireman, she grabbed the hose and turned the water on full blast. She aimed the gushing water at the point of contact maintained by the two dogs, and one of them yelped as the connection was broken.

"What happened?" I asked as my mother turned off the hose. "How come they were stuck like that?"

"Never mind!" she snapped. "Get ready for school."

My eighth-grade science teacher was the person whose image flashed into my mind, years later, when I discovered the word *curmudgeon*. Mrs. Graf was seldom friendly and always taught with strict authority. "Mr. Coronado, please stop tapping your pencil," she would order me when my light drumming became annoying. I nevertheless decided to ask her what had happened with Mickey and Blackie, since my mother would not explain and my sister cryptically revealed that someday I would know.

"And they were stuck together at the rear ends," I said to Mrs. Graf as I concluded what seemed to me to be a genuine scientific inquiry. Class had not quite started, and I took this opportunity to be individually enlightened. Somehow I knew, and I didn't know. I suspected I should have known more than I already did, but I barely knew enough not to embarrass myself. For instance, when the other boys laughed and made gestures with their hands that mimicked a rapid up and down motion while pretending to hold onto something tubular, I pretended to know what it was we were all laughing about. I had even heard the term, *jacking off*, but I did not discover the real meaning until many years later, after I was out of high school.

"They were mating," Mrs. Graf revealed, and dismissed me by focusing her attention on the day's lesson and the books and papers on her desk. I looked at her for many tense seconds.

When she noticed that I hadn't gone away, she glanced at me and asked, "Well, Mr. Coronado, what is it?"

"What's mating?" I asked with pure bred ignorance.

Mrs. Graf slowly took her glasses off, staring at me as if her brain was going through the process of discerning the degree of my naïvety.

"Ricky, they were making puppies," she said definitively.

Fear consumed me. Not because I still didn't understand, but because Mrs. Graf had only called me Ricky once before—and that was to wrongly accuse me of stealing some kid's military flashlight. I concluded that there was something serious and mysterious going on. I quickly gulped and thanked Mrs. Graf for her time.

"Hey, Mom!" I yelled as I walked into the house. "Guess what Mickey and Blackie were doing?" I went on, not waiting for an answer. "They were mating. They were making puppies!"

My mother and sister looked at each other and finally my mother asked, "Who told you that?"

"Mrs. Graf," I replied, "my science teacher."

"You asked your science teacher what Mickey and Blackie were doing?" my sister asked.

"Yeah," I replied and left it at that, not knowing if I was in trouble and feeling as if I had stumbled onto something too advanced. My mother and sister studied each other and then me.

"Go play, or do some homework," my mother forcefully suggested.

I went out to the backyard and called Mickey. She ran up to greet me and we sat on a wooden bench as I carefully but casually inspected her rear. "What were you two doing this morning, Mickey?" I asked. She looked up at me and tilted

her head, not understanding what I was saying. I threw the
tennis ball and urged her to "Get the ball, girl! Go on, get it!"
And she jumped off my lap and chased the bounding ball with
her usual tenacity. "She looks okay," I said to myself with a
degree of puzzlement. "I don't think she's hurt."

My sister came out to the backyard and beckoned me
inside. She was very serious in her tone, and I knew something was not right. "Let's talk," she suggested.

We went into her bedroom. She closed the door and sat on
the edge of the bed, instructing me to sit beside her. She
seemed to be searching for just the right thing to say. Then
she carefully asked, "Ricky, do you know where babies come
from?"

I looked at her with confusion and quickly decided that I
was being set up. "Of course I do," I replied with an air of
sophistication. "From a woman's stomach after she's been fat
for a long time."

"But do you know *how* a woman gets that way?" my sister
probed.

"Well, no," I said as I realized that my thinking had never
gotten that analytical.

My sister sat facing me, and with measured speech she
asked, "Are men like women?"

"What do you mean?" I asked as I became frightened at
her enigmatic questioning.

"Are men's bodies like women's?" she continued.

"Well, no," I gulped.

And she persisted, "Then how are they different?"

I could feel my forehead begin to ooze desperate beads of
sweat. "Well," I started, "men have a peepee, and women
don't."

"Right," my sister assured me. "Now pay close attention.
When a man and a woman want to have a baby, the man puts
his peepee in the woman's thing. A woman can't have a baby
without a man, and that's how they do it."

For a moment I felt like fleeing from the room. I felt as if
my sister was playing a dirty trick on me. "They do not," I
replied with a sense of disgust.

And she started again, this time in a scientific and
unemotional fashion. "Ricky, when a man and a woman want
to have a baby, the man gets on top of the woman and puts
his peepee in her thing for a little while, and then they have a

baby later on. That's what Mickey and Blackie were doing this morning. Only, they do it differently than people because they're dogs."

At this point, my uneasiness made me squirm as I replied, "That's ugly. Come on, Mónica. Why are you telling me this?"

"Because you need to know. You are old enough now, and it's time you knew," she answered. She continued with her explanation. "It's not ugly or disgusting, and someday you are going to do that, too."

I snapped my head back and moved away from my sister, resenting her forecast that I took as an accusation. "I will never do that," I persisted. "I swear to God, I will never do anything like that!"

Mónica smiled understandingly and assured me that someday I would indeed make babies like grown-ups do.

She dismissed me from her bedroom, and I quickly went outside to get Mickey. We retreated to my bedroom, and I could hear my mother and sister quietly conferring. Mickey gave me an affectionate lick as I said to her, "You know, Mickey, I didn't even know you were a woman."

# 20

I never got to play in any of the games, but I watched many of them. I was too young—in my early teens—to be considered as a possible participant. The players were knowledgeable and artificial in the ways of poker.

The group of players usually included my stepfather Ramón, my brother Hilario and his Spanish wife Chavela, my brother-in-law Santiago, and the next door neighbor, Bob Brown, who was also the town constable. There were others, but this core of sharps attended every game, and no game was considered memorable if it did not include these poker playing pillars.

The setting was indoors for the winter games—usually the kitchen table, and outdoors for the summer games. The summer games were played in our backyard. My stepfather had rigged up a luminous spotlight that hung from the eaves of the roof so the action could continue late into the night. I loved watching the summer poker games because the feeling of being outside in the night air had a comforting aspect to it. The San Joaquin valley heat would slowly dissipate and the relieving warmth provided an ambiance of kinship as fast friends laughed and played around a solitary wooden table that my stepfather had built.

Ramón was the oldest player and his poker skills were greatly respected. Like an actor, he had mastered a set of facial expressions to accompany his poker playing. His trademark was his ritual to summon luck. Whenever his poker chips dwindled to an amount that foreshadowed insolvency, Ramón would stand up as a hand was being dealt, and he would walk a complete circle around his chair and then sit down. He did not say or chant anything to confirm the act. He sat and smiled at each of the other players, and his expression announced that good things would now happen to him at the expense of the others. "*Ya*, you lucky now, huh, Ramón?"

Santiago would joke. Ramón would usually respond with a jovial "*Vamos a ver.* We see."

One time we tried to prevent this ritual by placing Ramón's seat against the back wall of the house and moving the table closer to that chair. But Ramón was too wily. It was the first thing he noticed as the game began to develop. "*¡Oh no no no no, ustedes no van a hacerme trampa. Ramón del Sol no está tonto!*" And then, for Mr. Brown's sake, "You guys not going to cheap me. Raymond del Sol not so stupid!" We all laughed as we moved the table to provide more open space.

Hilario was a good poker player. Having learned in the military the finer points of action and deception, he merged those qualities into his style of play. Hilario did not talk as much as the other players and talked more to Mr. Brown who spoke no Spanish at all. He was a seductive player and often commented on his cards by using one-word statements. Hilario's most effective mode of expression was a mysterious and elaborate delivery in a hushed voice as if whispering a secret. "Touuuuugh," he would slowly hiss and look at the other players with a snake-like charm. Other times he would sibilate "yeeesssss" or "*aaadiósssss.*" His wife Chavela, who was from the saucy streets of Madrid, would chide him after each exclamation and announce to the rest of the table that he was lying about his hand and that he had lied about many things for as long as she has known him. She would often switch to English to ask Constable Brown if "You no can put him in jail for make lie?"

Chavela was a crafty player and previous experience had taught her to beware all men, especially friendly poker-playing men. Her game was often marked by a nationalistic fervor that displayed itself anytime she won a hand. "*¡Arriba España!*" she would shout as she aggressively threw a winning hand down and scooped the chips towards her. Of course, the rest of the table did not allow this show of chauvinism to go unanswered, and each player soon had their own exhortation of nationalism whenever they won a hand. Ramón urged his home state in Mexico, "*¡Arriba Durango!*" Hilario, who was born in Texas, shouted, "*¡Arriba Tejas!*" Santiago, who, like Ramón, was from Mexico, had more of an agenda aimed at solidarity as he let out with "*¡Arriba Mexico!*" And finally, Bob Brown, one known to never back down, would shout, "Oklahoma is O.K.!"

Santiago played poker for sheer enjoyment; he was not as strategy-minded as the others; he did not pay much attention to cards that had been visibly played; and he seldom if ever raised a bet. His style seemed to suggest to just hang in there as long as possible and enjoy the company. He spoke very little English and much of his game was punctuated with Spanish. Whenever Mr. Brown spoke to Santiago, or Santiago had something to say to Mr. Brown, both looked at Hilario who automatically served as translator.

Mr. Brown played a sophisticated game of poker, and he had as much fun as anybody else. His laugh was the loudest and he was quite talkative. It did not matter that the game was predominantly conducted in Spanish. Bob Brown thought he was funny, and sometimes he was. He just didn't have the cognizance to know that Ramón, Chavela, and Santiago rarely understood his jokes. "I got a hand like a foot," he would quip, and Hilario and I were the only ones who laughed. Sometimes he would say, "I'm fixin' to deal the life of a bindlestiff to some poor folks," as he systematically arranged his cards prior to presenting an impressive hand.

I attended all of the games I could, but sometimes I just couldn't last as long as the players. There was the time Mrs. Brown casually walked into the backyard dressed in her nightgown, robe, and slippers, delivering Mr. Brown's morning cup of coffee. The previous night's game had gone on past dawn, and Mr. Brown was to be on duty in a short while. Another memorable gathering was during the Christmas holidays when a game, started the night before, was interrupted for all to attend morning church services, and then was continued as soon as the participants changed from their Sunday best and into card-playing clothes.

I never learned to play poker during that time. My attention was always focused on the interaction, in two languages, of friendly yet spirited competition. The hours spent around the wooden table outside, or the kitchen table inside, was a time of pure friendship and genuine communication.

## 21

It was one of the best profits I had ever turned. And I owed it all to my older brother Nacho. "Come on, Ricky. I'm hungry. Let's go get us some burgers," he invited.

"I don't have any money," I pitifully responded.

"Don't worry about it. It's my treat," he assured me.

We both requested a large soda pop, a large cheeseburger, and a large order of fries. "Is this for here or to go?" the lady asked as she took our order. "To go," Nacho answered.

I grabbed the big bag of food and beverages and we started home. Before my impulsive brother could get his car out of the parking lot of the hamburger joint, he requested his fries. "Put some ketchup on them for me." I sat with the warm food on my lap and the beverages wedged between my feet. By the time we made it to the first set of traffic lights that interrupted our journey home, Nacho requested a sip of his soda. He cruised through town slowly to see if there was anybody on the streets that he knew, but mainly so he could catch a red light at the next intersection. "Hand me my burger, Ricky," he said as we waited for the light to change.

The business section of town dissipated, and traffic lights gave way to simpler stop signs as we approached a more residential setting. "Hand me my soda pop," Nacho managed between savage bites of a disappearing burger. "Do I have any more fries left?" he garbled with his mouth half-full.

"No, you ate them all," I answered, and added, "And you don't have much soda pop left either."

"When are you going to eat your stuff?" he asked with a growing curiosity.

"I'm saving mine."

"For what, Thanksgiving?"

"No, not for Thanksgiving," I replied. "I'm waiting until we get home so I can watch television while I eat."

Nacho licked his fingers as his last bite of food descended into an urgent stomach. The dry sucking sound from the straw echoed that there was no more soda pop left. He commented with surprise, "Wow! I guess I finished everything I ordered."

"Yeah, you sure did," I said as I wadded up used napkins and other trash left by his carnage.

As the car pulled into the driveway, Nacho observed, "You still have everything you ordered."

"That's right," I responded. "I haven't touched a thing. I wonder what's on television right about now?"

He put the car in park and then casually requested, "Can I have a bite of your burger, Ricky?"

I was quick with my reprimand. "You see! You couldn't wait to get home to eat your stuff. Now you want some of mine."

"But I bought everything in the first place," he noted.

"So you bought it for me so you could take it from me?" I pointed out. This brought Nacho back to a degree of rationality. After a thoughtful moment, he started in from a different perspective.

"How about if I buy a bite from you?" he offered. My brother knew he had struck a passionate chord with me.

"Buy a bite?" I suspiciously asked.

"Yeah," he said matter-of-factly, "buy a bite."

"How about if I just sell you my burger?" I countered.

"Sell me your burger?" he slowly asked.

"Well, yeah. You want to buy a bite. Why not buy the whole burger?"

"But I bought you the burger in the first place."

"Yes, I know that. I was there. But it seems to me if you are willing to buy a bite, you might be interested in the whole thing."

"How much?"

"Oh, I don't know. Make me an offer. And start with what the burger cost in the first place."

My brother looked at me and realized I was serious. I, in turn, knew he was infected with the emotion of a buyer. "Okay, I'll give you eighty cents for the burger."

"Nope! I really can't take under a dollar for it."

"But it only cost *eighty cents* in the first place!"

"Really," I said with the honesty of a used-car salesman, "I can't take anything less than a dollar."

"What the hell do you mean you can't—" he began.

But I cut that part of the negotiations short by announcing, "You know, this burger will be too cold for either one of us to enjoy, so let's not drag this out."

"Why you little—," and he started towards me, but caught himself as I threatened to throw the food out of the car window.

"Okay, I'll give you a dollar for the burger," he said with resignation.

"It's a deal," I said. And the process of red-blooded American commerce was completed.

Before we got out of the car, I advertised while it was still a seller's market. "I'll sell you the fries, too, if you're interested."

Nacho looked at me with indignant eyes that expressed a bitterness and exploitation that was intolerable. But the words from his mouth asked, "How much?"

"Well, there are a couple of options here. I can sell you the fries *with* the soda pop for a much better price than you could get for just the fries alone."

"How much for just the damned fries!" he shouted with a taxed patience.

"One dollar, firm."

"One dollar? Ricky, what the he—"

But I blocked him again and interjected, "Or, you can buy the soda pop *and* the fries for a dollar-fifty. I'll even throw in the little packets of ketchup."

Nacho became quite philosophical as he muttered something about charity, greed, brotherhood, and other issues that I ignored. He handed over another dollar-fifty and I respectfully gave him everything that he had bought me.

"Now that that's over with, let's go inside and watch television," I suggested. And as we headed into the house I wondered aloud, "Do we have any baloney left?"

## 22

"Now that was fun!" he exclaimed.

"Boy, it sure was," I answered.

"Hey, Ricky, I wonder what it's like further down the river?" my older brother Nacho pondered.

We had been riding some mild rapids of the Kings River as it passed through the Reedley Beach. Our recreation soon developed a repetitious pattern of cruising down the river on our inner tubes, getting out and walking back to our picnic site, and reentering the river to embark on what had become too short a trip.

"Why don't we go down river a little more?" Nacho suggested as we broke for lunch.

"Well, I don't know—," I timidly began, not wanting to express that I was really satisfied with the mundane commuting pattern we had developed. I didn't have the heart or the nerve to quell my brother's gushing enthusiasm.

"Yeah!" he interrupted. "After lunch, let's go further down river." I could see that his excitement was growing.

"How much further do you want to go?" his young wife asked with concern as she passed out sandwiches. She knew my brother had an impressive history with fate.

"Oh, just a little bit more," Nacho vaguely offered as he caught on to the fact that others were now trying to intervene with what the gods already had in the books.

Nacho's infant son wiggled in his mother's arms as he reached out for his talking father. "Yeah, that's it," my brother started, "we'll just float down a little bit more—," and he was suddenly struck with a brainstorm. His eyes grew big. He looked at me with a jubilant fanaticism that made me feel uneasy. I tried to reciprocate, but my nerves flashed a warning sign to my brain.

"Riiiickyyyy," he started, as I tried to conceal a gulp that seemed to consume my throat. He delivered his thesis: "Let's float down to Vinecrest Rivertown Resort! It won't take us too long, an hour, hour-and-a-half at most. Carolyn can pick us up there." He continued with his oral defense: "It can't be that far down river. And there is plenty of daylight left. What time is it?" Carolyn shifted the baby boy on her lap as nervousness kept her from immediately responding.

"I don't know," I meekly hesitated, "tomorrow's the first day of school, and Mom will be mad if I'm not home in time to get ready."

"How long does it take to get ready for school?" my brother scoffed, having left such an institution at an early age, and without honors.

"Yes, Nacho," his wife added, "you know how upset your mother will get if we stay gone too long. Besides you have to work tomorrow." And in a final persuasive attempt: "And early, too!"

My sister-in-law and I knew we had been ineffective in convincing our singular audience. My baby nephew squirmed and laughed and waved his arms in the air, still lunging toward his father. I knew then that my brother had been successful in beginning a genetic heritage of impulsive ideas and fast-flowing adventures.

"See," Nacho urged, "even little Bobby thinks it's a good idea. Come on, Ricky, let's get ready. It'll be fun. Carolyn will pick us up in, oh, an hour, hour-and-a-half at the most. It's only two o'clock right now. We'll be home in plenty of time. I promise."

It was during these types of situations—when Nacho oozed with charisma and enthusiasm—that I became very existential. I wondered why God had made Nacho the one of my four brothers who was closest to me in age—even though there was almost a nine-year gap and a buffering sister between us. I also wondered why it seemed to be me who was always around when my brother was slapped with these aspirations. I theorized that my older brothers knew better than to get involved with Nacho in any endeavor. I thought about the time he suggested, "Let's go looking for Lost Cabin," a legendary hovel in the mountains with an alleged history of death and dying. Then there was the time he suggested we "...hop the train to Bakersfield and we'll take the bus back." I thought about the time *we* borrowed my mother's Ford Falcon to go to Foster's Freeze. All of these expeditions ended up involving the local authorities. Yes, I knew that all the world's great philosophers had been confronted with just these musings. I realized then the pain of living when one realizes too much. And I relented to my future as was written in the palm of my hand.

"Well, okay," I said as I looked at my sister-in-law for one last rebuttal.

"Nacho," she started, then realized she was wasting her breath. Little Bobby bobbed up and down and swung his body from side to side as if to affirm that his father certainly knew the meaning of life.

"Okay, this is what we're going to do." And Nacho outlined the itinerary. It was really quite simple, like all the other plans. We were to float down river until we got to Vinecrest Rivertown Resort. Carolyn and little Bobby would be there to meet us, and then we would go home. "We should be there at about, oh, three-thirty, four o'clock at the latest."

"Should we take our shoes?" I asked.

Nacho put his excitement on hold, and I knew he was about to reprimand me for asking a ridiculous question. "Ricky, Ricky, Ricky, Ricky. Now, why do we need to take our shoes? We are not going that far. Look, Vinecrest is only about five miles from Reedley, by road. Come on, let's get started." He hugged Carolyn and kissed her romantically. He held little Bobby and left wet kisses on his chubby face.

We entered the rushing water and waved as we disappeared down river. The first impulse to turn around choked me early into our journey. I noticed the river's rushing intensity had dramatically decreased, and I pointed this out to Nacho.

"That's because the river is winding, so the water naturally slows down," he explained. "It's like when a car slows down on a curve."

"You mean like we should have done on the way back from Foster's Freeze that time?" I asked, not expecting a direct answer, and having my expectation fulfilled.

"That was different," he pointed out, and added, "Now look ahead. You have to pay attention. There could be things sticking out of the river, and we don't want to run into anything."

As we floated down the river, I relaxed a little because I had discovered that I could stand up in the middle of the now slowly moving water and the water barely crested my shoulders.

"It's not that deep," I said.

"Of course not," Nacho responded. "That's why I knew this was a good idea. I know you don't know how to swim. I wouldn't put you in a dangerous situation. Mom would kill me."

I thought about reminding him of our aborted train trip and why our plans that day had taken a tumultuous turn. And I wanted to ask him if he remembered how many people became involved in our search for Lost Cabin as they searched for us. But the peaceful surroundings had pacified my apprehensions, and the warm sun comforted me like a security blanket.

"How long have we been in the water?" I asked after what I thought was the time of our arrival.

Nacho had been assiduously studying the river and was annoyed with my utterances. "We haven't been in that long," he answered, and then quickly delivered his next inspiration. "I'm going up on land ahead where the river bends, and I'll meet you on the other side. That way I can get a general idea of where we are. You'll be okay by yourself. Just keep floating. After you round the bend, whistle so I can know if you passed by or not."

"Okay," I said, and I knew it would do no good to express my growing concern.

"Come ashore, seal pup!" Nacho yelled as he startled me from my peaceful meandering and hurled rocks all around my floating vessel.

"What happened?" I asked, as I dragged my wet body and inner tube to the riverside.

"I talked to some kid, and he said Vinecrest is just down river a bit," Nacho announced.

"What kid? Where is he?" I asked as my eyes searched for the informant.

"Some kid back there," Nacho obscurely offered. "He said we're not that far away." He knew I was growing uneasy. But I said nothing and neither did he. Somehow my tendency to always expect the worse never hindered him from putting into action the ideas that snagged onto his mind and firmly sunk their fomenting hooks there. "Well, let's shove," he ordered. And we were floating towards our predetermined goal once again.

"Well, we're down river a bit," I reminded him after I determined that the sun had noticeably moved since we had reentered the river.

"Reeelax, Ricky," Nacho soothed, "we'll see what's going on after we round this bend."

As we proceeded, I spotted an elderly man fishing, and I became alive with hope. "Hey, there's a guy!" I blurted out excited at spotting a fatherly figure who would certainly know what was what.

"Hey, mister," Nacho asked as we neared the angler, "do you know how far it is to Vinecrest Rivertown Resort?"

"Vinecrest?" the man asked, slowly scratching the side of his face and striking the pose of one deep in thought. "Vinecrest is just around the next bend," he finally concluded as we floated by.

The next bend came and went. The bend after that welcomed us and saw us off down more river. We experienced the river as it bent to the right. And we floated through parts of the river that wound to the left.

"Did he say how many bends until we get to Vinecrest?" I asked. "Or did he say, 'just around *the* next bend?'"

Nacho calmly responded, "Don't worry, Ricky, I think I see somebody up ahead on shore. See?"

Up ahead indeed, in the nebulous distance, was the shadowy figure of somebody standing in the trees and staring into the water. As we approached the figure, we came to discover that no informative assistance would be offered. It was a horse. It stood on the riverbank blankly staring at our sagging figures in wending vessels.

"Well, I guess he won't tell us much," Nacho observed, and he greeted the silent spectator as we passed by. "Heeellooo, I'm Mr. Ed." I didn't laugh as hard as Nacho did. Although I made a good effort to fake it.

"Something's wrong, Nacho," I started. "Somehow we missed Vinecrest. We've been floating for too long. I think we're lost. We went the wrong way." And the panic overturned my patience. "The sun is starting to set and it will be dark pretty soon. We have only seen two people and a horse since we left Reedley Beach. I have to start school tomorrow,

and Mom's going to kill me for being out so late on a Sunday.
I think we should—."

"Ricky, shut up!" Nacho ordered. "Now stop sniveling.
We're okay. We're almost there, I know it. Now just wait a
minute while I get my bearings."

"We never had any bearings when we left," I argued.

"Quiet! I need to check something out." He looked up at
the position of the sun. Then he turned to look back at the
river behind us. He scanned both banks and the land beyond
them. He laughed and announced, "You know, I sure don't
recognize anything that looks like it might be close to
Vinecrest. But we're all right," he quickly confirmed.

"I'm scared," I said.

"You're always scared," he reminded me. "Besides, what
are you scared of? The water's not that deep. It's not cold.
We're still on the same river. It's not like we're driving and
took the wrong road. Relax, we're cool."

As dusk offered less light, we spied a man and a woman
fishing. Nacho decided we would go ashore here and glean
some first-hand information, concluding that if we confronted
our informants directly as opposed to information dispensed
to us as we floated by, what we were told would be much more
accurate.

"Vinecrest?" the couple asked in harmony. The man
slowly stroked the back of his neck and the woman looked
into the horizon with faraway eyes as they both thought
about the question presented to them. The man started,
"Vinecrest, is, just around the next swooping bend. There will
be a couple of little bends, but then there will be a big curvy
bend in the river, and after that, you should come to
Vinecrest." The woman remained silent, but nodded her head
affirmatively.

Nightfall conveyed to both of us that we would not even
recognize the big curvy bend should destiny place us in the
middle of it.

"Okay," Nacho relented, "maybe we should get out and
walk."

"We're lost, huh?" I asked, not wanting to hear the truth,
especially Nacho's version of it.

He grew annoyed and snapped, "We aren't lost, Ricky!
Now just wait a minute." And he thought for many minutes

as we continued down a dark waterway. "Let's hit the beach here. I need to figure something out," Nacho directed.

My brother emerged from his personal think tank as we sat on the dark riverbank. "Okay, let's just start walking in the direction of the sun—," he attempted.

"The sun's not even up anymore," I helplessly protested.

"Ricky, Ricky, Ricky, Ricky," Nacho replied with a Cheshire-cat-like grin, "I mean where the sun went down. We'll just head west and see where we end up. Quit worrying."

"I told you we should of brought our shoes," I reminded him. There was no response. We abandoned our inner tubes and climbed up a steeper embankment as we started our foot journey. Minutes later, we were walking through organized rows of grape vineyards.

"Now this is a good sign," Nacho assured. "We should get to a farmhouse or something soon."

We biblically wandered through the fertile rows, and faith eventually granted a more meaningful sign of civilization—an asphalt road. "I wonder what road this is," Nacho said. "I think I've picked around here before."

I was not interested in his past; rather, I was very concerned about my future. "Now which way?" I asked as we looked north into a darkness that revealed little, and then south into a comparable void.

"Let's go this way," Nacho suggested as we started south on the country road.

"Why this way?" I asked.

Nacho stopped suddenly and confronted me with, "Okay, should we go the other way? It's up to you."

I recognized this pattern from previous expeditions and it always ended the same way. "No," I relented, "let's just keep going this way." But by now I had developed my own cynical touch and added, "Tijuana is probably just up ahead."

"If a car comes by, step off the road and I'll try to flag it down," Nacho advised.

The first car flew by us in revelry, beer cans spewing out from both sides. "I don't think they would have been much help," Nacho pointed out. A few minutes later I noticed an approaching vehicle. Before Nacho could begin his flagging down gesticulations, the car was slowing and a spotlight of authority splashed on us.

The vehicle pulled off to the side of the road and the voice from inside asked, "Are you the boys that everybody's looking for on the river?"

"I guess so," Nacho answered. "We've been floating down the river since two o'clock."

"Yep, you're the ones then," the sheriff informed us. "Get in and I'll take you back to the station. Your wife's waiting for you there."

"Who's looking for us?" I asked, knowing that my mother would not be too pleased with this adventure.

"Well," the sheriff began with a chuckle, "there are people searching for you in three counties: Fresno, Tulare, and Kings. We weren't sure if you abandoned the river and started walking or if you were still on the river. So there are people looking all over."

"Wow!" Nacho exclaimed as he seemed to be proud of the activity our journey had created.

"Your mother's pretty upset," the sheriff continued, "but we kept telling her that we didn't think you drowned because the river never gets past five feet in depth this time of year."

"Is this going to make the news?" Nacho asked with perverse anticipation.

"Oh, it should," the sheriff casually replied as the cruiser pulled up to the station.

Outside were other deputies with cups of coffee. Carolyn stood off to one side holding little Bobby. She was a mature woman for her young years, and as she hugged her husband and ran her fingers through his thick hair, she held back a volume of tears that expressed her relief. "We gotta get home, honey," she said.

"What are all the cars about?" I asked as we approached my mother's house and the house we all shared.

"Oh, some friends and neighbors are taking care of Mom. She didn't take this as well as everybody else has," Carolyn calmly answered.

I was the first one to walk into a hero's welcome. My mother came running down the hallway to seize the son she thought she had lost. She smothered me with her bosom and cried enormous tears of joy thanking the Lord for my safe return. She hurled a resentful look at Nacho as he assured the guests that we were all right and that we had merely misjudged the windiness of the river.

"Oh, my son, my son," my mother cried as she squeezed my limp body. Nacho excused himself, attributing his hasty exit to a forthcoming workweek. My mother stroked my hair, and someone handed her a towel to dry me off some more. She rocked me in her arms for a few moments as the helpful visitors began to return to their homes. "You okay, *m'ijo?*" she asked. Then she offered, "Take a quick shower and let's see if Foster's Freeze is still open."

## 23

As we walked, we talked of many things. Football was the main topic of discussion. And even though we commented on the short dress that Ophelia Reyes had worn the day before, and homework that was due but not yet done, we returned to our current passion of football. The Thanksgiving weekend had just passed, and the buzz of Christmas started us into a discussion about possible Christmas gifts. We debated the merits of a football that had Gale Sayers' signature etched in it as opposed to one with Roman Gabriel's.

Our briskly moving feet crunched the frozen ground beneath us; our intent was to warm our bodies by maintaining a steady pace during the one-mile trek to school. It would be the only time Jesse Colmenares and I could spend together until school let out later that day. Our Freshman year in high school had disappointed us from the beginning when we discovered that we did not have a single class together. Our shock was intensified when we further analyzed our new schedules and realized that we did not even have lunch at the same time—I had first lunch and Jesse had second lunch. So we decided to walk to and from school to catch up with what was happening in each other's lives.

"I would rather have a football with Gale Sayers' autograph on it," I rebutted after Jesse declared that a Roman Gabriel inscribed football was much better; his main point of contention was that "Gabriel *throws* the football, and with a nice tight spiral. Sayers just *carries* the football."

We approached the school grounds from the back, first crossing the baseball field and then the practice football field adjacent to the gymnasium. As we made our way into the hub of the campus and our lockers, we often met small groups of students: smokers, *pachucos*, and guys who loved auto shop.

I was about to make what I thought was a brilliant point, that Sayers could run and make everybody miss tackles, that

he could *carry* the ball *through* eleven guys who were trying
to knock his block off. We were faithful to our respective arguments, and our voices rose as we attempted to drive a point
home. I did not hear the interrupting voice, but Jesse did.

"*Yyyy,* a Chicano with a *gabacho. Yyyy,* that's bad," hissed
a *pachuco* who was leaning against the gymnasium wall with
his comrades.

I kept walking, deep in thought over my next valid statement concerning my football idol. But I quickly discovered
that Jesse was no longer walking beside me. His attention
was focused on the social commentator with the black, slick-
backed hair, black pants, and black pointed shoes. Jesse
approached the human buttress and his three companions as
I stopped and turned to see what direction our discussion was
taking.

"Did you have something to say to us?" Jesse asked the
vocal one. I could tell by his direct manner of address that
this was not to be a pleasant exchange.

"Yeah, I do," the keynote speaker responded as he
relieved his leaning body from the wall and reiterated his
point. "I said a Chicano with a *gabacho.* That don't look so
good to me."

Jesse was quick. "Then don't look!"

I could feel my legs start to tremble as the other leaners
extricated themselves from the wall and formed a semi-circle
in front of us. Jesse stood his ground, his black eyes challenging the student in front of him.

"Don't talk to me that way, *ese.* I'll beat your fuckin' ass
so bad, you won't never want to hang out with a *pinche gabacho* again!"

"Then do it now, *ese,*" Jesse replied as he finished with a
taunting tone.

"Why don't you let fatboy talk," the *pachuco* invited. "I
got nothing against you, you're a Chicano."

I cleared my throat and with blatant fear and humility
offered, "I'm a Chicano, too. I just don't look like it." I didn't
have an explanation for being lighter-skinned. But I wanted
to tell the paisano that my parents were born in Mexico; from
Tamaulipas and Chihuahua. That I didn't have an accent like
he or Jesse, probably because I watched too much television:
"My Three Sons," "The Beverly Hillbillies," and "Gunsmoke."
I wanted him to know that I picked grapes and even spent a

winter pruning and tying vines, and that only Mexicans did that kind of work. I wanted to tell him that I knew how to cook menudo. I wanted him to hear me sing songs by Javier Solís and José Alfredo Jiménez. But somehow I couldn't say anything more.

Jesse of course took control before anybody could offer any explanations or solutions. "If you got something against him, you got something against me." As he spoke, he straightened the fingers of his right hand letting his books and binder splash to the ground. Within seconds, Jesse had two fists calmly waiting at his sides. I began to sweat and wanted to leave.

The *pachuco* came to a resourceful conclusion. "I don't want to fight you here, *ese*. We might get kicked out of school. Meet us in the parking lot after school. And make sure you bring some friends."

I liked this suggestion. It allowed for us to escape after school and have my mother drive us each morning and pick us up each afternoon from then on. But Jesse was a serious student. He was like that when we played football—he made up the plays because he was always the quarterback. I was disturbed when he announced to the four members of the opposite team that we take care of the matter here and now.

"Let's just get this over with," Jesse suggested. "If you four *changos* think you can kick our ass, do it now. We can't meet you after school, we work." And then he offered even more options to the enemy. "We walk this way every morning and every afternoon after school. You can find us here and get us after school if you want to. We aren't going to meet you anywhere." As he picked up his books, he kept staring at the four encroachers, never taking his eyes off theirs.

The main speaker expelled a nervous chuckle and warned, "Don't ever let us catch you alone or you'll be sorry, *ese*." They strutted onto the main part of the campus as Jesse looked around.

We stood there for a moment as we forgot about football, Ophelia Reyes, homework, and the cold valley air. "We still have time before school starts," Jesse said. "Let's just wait here until we hear the first bell." We leaned against the gymnasium wall, and after a few quiet minutes, we resumed our discussion about whose name on a football offered the most inspiration.

# 24

As adolescence grabbed hold of my attitude, I found it more and more difficult to understand my mother's point of view—about anything. It was quite a dramatic time for us, and we got along like a married couple who knew it wasn't working out.

My mother constantly did not know what to do with me. She couldn't talk to me. I was acting strangely. My grades were dropping. Furthermore, I developed a rather sarcastic way of responding to everything she had to say to me. Since she could not come up with practical solutions as to how to remedy her renegade son, I offered one.

"How about if I move in with Mónica and David?" I suggested one day after a heated discussion about responsibility. "I would be out of your way, and you and Ramón could finally enjoy some peace and quiet. You wouldn't have to worry about me or spend money on me." I proceeded with my case. "I only have two more years of school left before I leave anyway."

"And you expect Mónica and David to take care of you?" she asked unconvinced.

"No," I replied. "I expect me to take care of me. I can work on weekends. I already know how to wash and iron my own clothes. I really think I can take care of myself without being a burden to them."

It was a sad departure for both of us, but we knew it was for the good of our future relationship. The emotion of leaving my mother's house was attenuated by the fact that not only would I be living with my sister and her husband, but that the three of us would be moving to an entirely new world: We were moving to Lake Tahoe.

As we headed down Echo Summit, we admired the beautiful blue lake. David carefully maneuvered the old pickup truck as it made its way over the icy road. "I'm glad we didn't have to chain up," he said, concentrating on the winding road ahead of him. The snow was quite high by now. Winter was firmly in place, and a new year had been born only days earlier.

All of our belongings were piled in the back of the pickup, and the journey from the San Joaquin valley to Lake Tahoe was coming to an end. We turned the corner of a residential neighborhood and started up a small hill. The old truck struggled halfway up the hill and quit as we slid back about fifty yards. We tried again. After half a dozen attempts at cresting the hill, David got out of the truck and stood in front of it. He assessed the incline and the snow level while Mónica and I sat in the warm cab and watched.

"He's going to have to chain up just to get to the top," I said.

"No, I don't think so," Mónica responded. "The snow on the road doesn't seem that deep."

"I'm going to have to chain up," David said, reaching behind the seat to pull out the tire chains. "The snow on the road is too deep to make it all the way to the top."

I offered some smugness to my sister who thanked me by punching me on the arm. I reacted by locking my left arm around her head and rapidly filing her pate with the knuckles of my right hand. She screamed. I laughed. An irritated David told us to behave.

Before we were able to settle into our cozy little mountain cabin, we discovered that we would have much to learn about our new environment. The cabin sat on the back of a long, deep lot. The entrance was a dirt driveway that made a complete loop in front of the house. The snow was piled about three feet high everywhere but on the street. We could barely get the truck far enough onto the property and scarcely close enough to the snow-capped dwelling. Before we could unload the truck, we had to shovel our way back to the cabin.

David immediately sensed that the business of shoveling snow was a tedious one, especially since we did not yet own a snow shovel. We were clearing our way with a hoe and a dust pan. He did not like the idea of only being able to squeeze onto his property and having to trudge the remaining distance to the cabin through deep snow.

"Let's go see how much a snowblower costs," David suggested a few days after we had moved in. He had experienced a couple of days of working at his new job delivering propane to homes throughout the city. He had seen the results of a snowblower and knew immediately that was what our new place needed.

"I got it used," David began, introducing the snowblower to us, "but it'll do the job."

He yanked the rope that set the machine into motion. It rumbled from side to side as Mónica and I stared at the chugging object. David pushed a lever and the masticating prongs at the front of the machine began to digest the snow and expel it from a chute to the side of the circular driveway. After a few minutes, he let the machine idle and walked back to where my sister and I stood, two puffy figures clad in layers of shirts, sweaters, and jackets.

"You want to try it, Ricky?" David offered. "It's easy to use, and besides, I'm going to need your help in keeping this driveway clear. We don't want to lug groceries all the way up from the street."

David demonstrated as he slowly pushed the lever into gear and the machine resumed its swath of consumption. The snowblower could clear a path about two feet wide, so many passes had to be made on the looping driveway. Subsequent snowstorms would require more snowblowing throughout the winter.

The remainder of that winter, David worked, I went to school, and Mónica was a housewife. We did not make many friends because the snow made it more convenient for us to stay home enjoying a warm fire and hot chocolate. We stuck together and learned what we could about our new community. Around the end of March, as the persistent winter was reluctantly giving way to a hatching spring, we learned more.

I yanked on the rope to start the snowblower. While the old, dependable machine warmed up, I stood with my hands in my pockets and looked up into the lazily falling snowflakes. The stillness of winter and the muffled but rhythmic chugs of the cold machine lulled me into a state of pensive meditation.

"WHATCHA LOOKIN' AT, BUGEYES!" a harsh, witchlike voice yelled into my ear.

My moment of thought was shattered by Mónica, who had sneaked out to the tool shed solely for the purpose of startling me. "What are you doing out here?" I bitterly asked. "Aren't there any soap operas on television?"

Mónica playfully pushed me and replied, "Oh, come on Ricky, you know I don't watch those things." She continued as I made final adjustments on the machine, "Besides, I'm bored. I feel like I have been cooped up in this cabin for weeks."

"Well, you have," I replied. "You could have cabin fever."

"What's cabin fever?"

"Some guys I met at school were talking about it. They said it's where you start to feel like you're going nuts because of all the snow."

"Yeaaah," Mónica said, slowly nodding her head in agreement.

"They said last winter this one guy killed his wife and kids, even the family pet, because of cabin fever."

"Really? It does kind of make sense. You know, I was sitting in the house reading, and for some reason I just started getting mad and frustrated and I didn't know what to do."

"So you decided to sneak out here and scare the crap out of me, is that it?" Mónica laughed, slapping my arm while I put the machine in gear and began my snow clearing.

"I think I'm going to stay out here for a few minutes," Mónica informed me as I pulled away. "David will be home in a little while."

I cleared the entrance to the driveway first, so David could at least make it onto the property. As I started around the rest of the driveway, my sister watched. On the second pass, I noticed her mouth moving but could hear no words because the noise of the snowblower grew louder. I pushed the lever into neutral and guided the machine closer to her.

"What are you flapping your jaws about?"

"I want to try that," she shouted over the noise of the machine as she pointed to it.

"Try this?" I said with a disbelieving tone and also pointing to the machine. I laughed for an exaggerated amount of time—until a huge snowball exploded on top of my capped head. "I can't let you try this," I said, brushing the snow off my head.

"Why not?"

"Because you don't know how to use it," I explained. "Mónica, this machine has a highly sophisticated nature to it and you don't."

"Oh, come on, Ricky, it can't be that difficult. Come on, let me try it."

"Look, Mónica, this is not a toy," I said with assumed authority. "Besides, I need to finish this so David can make it all the way in."

"Just let me try it for a few minutes," she persisted.

"All right, but not too long, and follow the path I've already started," I instructed. I put the machine in gear and it slowly started displacing the snow again. Mónica grabbed onto the handles and headed down the driveway. I looked up into the thick gray sky and contemplated the silence of the descending flakes for a few moments. When I returned to my physical reality, I noticed Mónica hunkering over the machine studying whatever instructions were written on the gear box. She grabbed one of the handles of the snowblower, and with her free hand pulled the lever back toward her. The snowblower went into reverse. As Mónica manipulated the lever again, it jumped forward. She repeated this motion a few times. I realized I would have to relieve her of her duty.

As I approached my sister, she knew I was about to take away her fun. "Wait a minute," she said. "Watch this." Mónica put the machine in gear and, stiffening her legs, she let the machine pull her. "Wheeeee, I'm skiing," she gleefully announced, letting the machine pull her towards the cabin.

I was not impressed with her imagination, and I gruffly cut in to regain control of her new ski machine. I was not mean to my sister, ever. And when I pushed her aside, I had not expected her to fall on her face and slide a few feet. I yelled out a hasty "sorry" and continued with my work while she brushed the snow from her parka.

The machine trudged on and I began my final pass on the snow-covered driveway. I had forgotten about Mónica for a few seconds, but I was quickly reminded of her when she separated me from the machine with a tackling bear hug.

"What are you doing?" I gasped as we struggled on the snowy ground.

"Next time, say you're sorry when you do something like that," she replied, holding onto me and trying to push my face into the powdery surface.

"Mónica, the snowblower's still going. I'm sorry. Now let me go." She jumped up, kicked snow at me, and ran after the slowly-moving machine that was now headed for a clump of trees.

By now my vindictive juices were flowing, and I ran after my sister, pushing her from behind and sending her bobsledding into a snowbank. I looked up just in time to see the snowblower crash head-on into a solitary tree. The silence seemed eerie for a few seconds as I stood dumbly looking at the coalesced tree and machine. I did not have much time to think about what had just happened, as my sister executed another ambush and again knocked me to the slippery landscape.

"Mónica—," I attempted as we rolled around on the snow-padded ground, "I think we broke the snowblower."

"*You* broke the snowblower!" she accused as she threw blows that my layered body absorbed.

I wrestled myself from her grip and stood up to inspect the dead machine. When I pulled it away from the tree, the front plate that served as a guard from the gnawing blades fell to the ground. Mónica laughed hysterically. Snow covered her entire body, and she looked like a little white polar bear as she continued to taunt me.

I attempted to pull the lever into neutral, and the entire gear box fell from the frame of the snowblower, partially sinking in the snow. Her shrieking laughter continued to pierce the icy silence. With one last effort, I tugged on the rope to start the machine, only to have it snap while the snowblower burped some career-ending sounds.

I only let Mónica pelt me with one more snowball before I chased her retreating figure. I tackled her and began smearing snow all over her face. We struggled for minutes. At times I would have her seemingly defeated, then she would break loose with a body punch or a handful of snow to my face or down my back. She was a dirty fighter, and she effectively employed upper body blows and lower body kicks. We were both surprised when David suddenly appeared as the arbitrator to our disagreement. We hadn't heard him drive up.

"What the hell do you guys think you're doing?" he asked, holding both Mónica and me at arm's length by the scruff of our parkas.

As we looked at one another, Mónica began, "We were snowblowing."

"Yeah, we were snowblowing," I repeated.

"Well, where's the snowblower?" David asked.

We again looked at one another, and Mónica and I popped with ridiculous laughter.

"Where's the damn snowblower?" David demanded. Our laughter subsided momentarily. Then we pointed to the machine at the base of the tree. David looked over at the snowblower and fired angry looks back at us.

"I'm going to go start dinner, honey," Mónica said, slithering away from any more questions.

"Come on, Ricky, let's see if we can fix this thing," David said, a hint of frustration in his voice. As we walked towards the totaled snowblower, David shook his head. "I don't believe you guys." He had barely uttered the final sound of his statement when a snowball splattered on his backside.

Mónica ran inside. The slamming of the door caused a small avalanche of snow to fall from the roof of the cabin onto the partially cleared driveway.

David grinned slightly. As he hunched over the moribund machine, he muttered, "She must have cabin fever."

## 25

"Have you ever been drunk before, Ricky?" Paul asked.

"Oh, yeah, a few times," I answered, not wanting to appear unsophisticated to my new friends and adding a mature, "More times than I care to admit."

In fact, I had never been drunk in my life. I had seen drunks. And I had heard drunks. I had even touched drunks to help them out of a car or into a house. These experiences were all the courtesy of my father. But, at eighteen, I could not say that I had ever known what it was like to be drunk. Of course, my companions, Paul and Tony, were veterans, even if they were a year younger than me; they had been drunk on many occasions.

Tony's older brother bought us a big bottle of whiskey and delivered it to us while we waited at the side of the liquor store. Paul went in and bought a variety of non-alcoholic mixers. We then walked to my house before going to the local high school basketball game.

I lived with my sister and her husband, who were out for the evening. We would have the entire place to ourselves, but we only intended to drink there and then walk to the game. It made me feel good that throughout our planned evening there would be no driving, especially since the snow had grown deep, and the only document involving driving held among the three of us was one learner's permit. The idea of not involving vehicles in our night of imbibing made the venture seem harmless.

Paul and Tony casually mixed their own drinks. I awkwardly and self-consciously stepped up to the kitchen counter to make my first alcoholic beverage. I glanced at each of my friends' glasses to see how much ice and mix they threw in. It looked simple enough, so I tossed in a few ice cubes, pouring the whiskey until the glass was half-full.

"That's going to be a good drink," Tony observed.

"You won't need too many of those," Paul added.

"Yeah," I said, slightly puffing my chest, "that's how I like my drinks." I complemented the drink with some soda pop and took a big gulp without stirring the mixture. Paul and Tony looked at each other with suspicion, and then took equally big drinks from their own tumblers.

I didn't feel the effects of the first drink as fast as I expected to, so I quickly mixed a second one before my companions could finish their first. Paul rose next to mix a second cocktail for himself. This time I paid close attention to his method. He freshened the glass with more ice then poured in about two inches of the alcohol. He then filled the remainder of the glass with soda pop and stirred his creation. He took a test-taster's sip and nodded as he admired his own talent. When Tony made his drink, I noticed he poured in about the same amount of liquor as Paul had. I had poured what looked to be at least twice that amount in my drinks. As I slowly sipped my second cocktail, I grew slightly nervous about what might happen to me.

While we fondled our third round of drinks, Paul looked at his watch and said, "Wow! The game starts in thirty minutes. We better get going. It'll take about that long to walk there." We spilled our beverages into our gaping mouths and prepared ourselves to walk the mile-and-a-half over snow-covered roads.

The frigid evening air felt relieving to my flushed face. I stumbled a little as I put on my gloves and proceeded after my cautiously moving friends down the street. Shortly after we embarked on our journey to the high school, I began to feel a significant change in my perception. The alcohol influenced my senses and made me respond to the world in a different light.

The three of us walked down the street, shoulder to shoulder, each of us with our hands in our coat pockets. A car slowly approached from behind and honked a warning sound as it trudged over the snowy roads.

"What's he honking about?" Paul asked.

"Just some punks going to the game," Tony answered.

"If anybody else does that, let's nail 'em with snowballs," I added. "Real hard-packed ones."

When we approached the school, another passing car honked at us. We were so relaxed; it seems that we were ambling all over the street instead of remaining on the side as when we first set out.

"Get a job, asshole!" I yelled, and I quickly packed a snowball and hurled it at the departing car. Paul and Tony remained neutral in this exchange. They seemed to focus most of their attention on navigating through the increasingly growing darkness.

"Okay, you guys, let's maintain when we're paying to get in. Don't blow it, or they'll kick us out," Paul advised us.

By now I had become much more of an outgoing individual than my normal self. In fact, I had become many outgoing individuals. I had thrown snowballs at as many cars as I could while we crossed the school parking lot, and I had flipped off a few citizens who didn't like the way I was having fun.

"What if they say, 'aaaaaaammmmmmmm, you been drinkinnnnng, I'm gonna tell your mommyyyy.' Then what do I do?" I drunkenly and playfully slurred as we approached the gymnasium.

"Come on, dude, maintain until we get in," Paul urged.

Once we were inside, we directed our efforts to the uppermost bleacher seats where nobody would be sitting behind us. I struggled with my balance as I carefully and waveringly climbed the bleacher steps and seats in an effort to reach the summit that my companions had already attained.

Before I sat down, I stood at the top of the bleachers and struck a pose of conquest. I stood there, my head only a few feet from the ceiling. I held up an imaginary sword or flag or whatever it is that conquerors hold up to claim something in the name of somebody or someplace. "I claim this land in the name of Sweet Georgia Brown. Long live the queen."

Half the crowd from our side of the bleachers had turned around and were looking up at me. Paul and Tony were tugging at my pants. As they nervously laughed, they pleaded with me to sit down.

I looked down at the staring half of the crowd that had turned to acknowledge me. Holding my arms extended in front of me with my hands open, I gave a sweeping and bleary-eyed look at the congregation, and with papal authority said, "The mass is ended. Go in peace." I let out a bitter drunken laugh as I climbed down to sit between my two friends.

"Man, you're going to get us kicked out of here," Paul admonished me while I wiggled from side to side as I sat down, imitating a nesting bird.

"Do you get like this every time you get drunk, Ricky?" Tony asked. His left shoulder was slightly in front of my right shoulder, and he applied pressure as needed while I rocked forward and backward.

I looked at my concerned friend and said with inebriated eloquence, "Wassa matter, Tony, bro, methinks youthinks I gonna faa down go boom! Huh, Tony? That's what you two mugs think, huh?"

Paul and Tony leaned forward slightly and looked at each other, expressing only with their eyes a dubious concern.

I watched some of the game. But I was a childish drunk. My attention span was truncated as my eyes and thoughts wandered from those who were watching the game to the cheerleaders, or to scanning the ceiling of the gymnasium for something to grab onto and possibly swing down from. I threw spit wads at a few people. But when I hit the star wrestler of our school, Paul and Tony latched onto my wrists and began to discipline me.

Paul pleaded, "Ricky, you're going to get us kicked out of here if you don't settle down. Now quit throwing spit wads, please? Okay?"

"Wwwwpppphhhh," was the sound that issued from my mouth when I indiscreetly launched the wet wad of paper that was being prepared for my next pitch. The soggy projectile landed between two girls who looked at it and screeched at the horror of the intrusive salivary blot that rudely took up the space between them.

As half-time approached, Paul and Tony decided to escort me outside. Once we were in the frosty air, I felt a sense of refreshing freedom, but it was mainly because Paul and Tony had released their grips from my arms as they were diverted by a group of familiar girls discussing the logistics of an impending party.

I'm not too sure how the fight started, or if it was even a fight. A couple of days after our outing, as we sat in my bedroom, Paul and Tony laughingly gave me an account of my pugilistic efforts, along with other events from that evening.

"We aren't sure what happened, Ricky," Paul began. "You did get in a hassle with Rocky Riley, but he let you off easy and just slapped you around a little bit until we convinced him that you were too ripped to know who you were or what you were doing." Paul continued, "It was kind of funny, because he did throw you over his truck and—"

"Wait a minute!" I interrupted. "You mean I tried to fight somebody, and Rocky Riley of all beasts?" I was amazed at what my friends were telling me. But it is true that I don't remember where a chunk of time went that night. And my jaw and chin were both sore. And I had noticed a tear in one of my pants' legs. I also was aware of a road burn and dried blood on that leg. "Wow," I said with some confusion, "I really don't remember that."

"Oh, it was great!" Tony offered. "Rocky had to yank you out of his truck; he doesn't know how you got in. Nothing was broken, and he was sure he locked it. He likes that truck more than his girlfriend. Anyway, he grabbed you by the front of your jacket and yanked you out and threw you up against the car parked next to his truck and asked you what you were doing in there."

"Where were you guys?" I asked.

"Oh, we were looking for you, and we only found you when we heard there was a fight in the parking lot," Paul explained.

"I think you were just sleeping when Rocky found you," Tony continued, "but when he asked you what you were doing in his truck and you said 'Waiting for your girlfriend,' he popped you a good one. Is your jaw sore?"

"Yeah, as a matter of fact it is," I said, my ego feeling a little bruised.

"How about your chin?" Paul asked, smirking as he did.

"Yeah, my chin is sore, too," I said, my face growing warm with embarrassment.

"That was when Rocky nailed you with a vicious uppercut to the chin," Tony narrated.

Paul added in the analytical tone of a boxing broadcaster, "It was a pretty punch."

"Thanks," I grimly responded, "I'm honored to be the recipient of such a gesture."

"But go on, Tony," Paul urged as he openly laughed in my face, a mockery I admittedly deserved.

"Wait!" I protested. "How come you knuckleheads let this happen to me? Why didn't you just take me home or something?"

"We tried," Tony said. "We just lost you. And when we found you, you were surrounded by a bunch of burly guys who wanted to use you as a tackling dummy."

"You're really lucky, Ricky," Paul added with serious assessment.

"Yeah, you are," Tony agreed. "One of them said something about taking you out to the woods and tying you up to a tree and throwing snowballs at you. After they'd pantsed you, of course!"

"Ouch," I miserably responded.

"But, I had the nerve to get you out of it, Ricky," Tony valiantly informed me.

"Thanks again," I said, not really wanting to hear the rest, but knowing I would.

"I spoke up," Tony began, "and I said to Rocky and his gorillas that you were too drunk to know what you were doing, and that we all knew that anybody that wanted to mess with Rocky *had* to have something wrong with him, and Rocky thought about it for a second and liked what he heard." Tony paused for a moment, caught his breath, and continued. "But before he let you go, he asked you how you got in his truck, and you—," Tony stopped as his convulsing, laughing body prevented him from continuing the narrative. Paul's shaking body and howling laughter made me feel I was an outstanding representative of foolishness. He then wiped joyous tears from his eyes and looked at Tony. Tony, in return, looked back causing them both to re-engage in a fit of extreme merriment. Paul offered the palm of his right hand and Tony slapped it. "Anyway," Tony attempted, stifling chuckles as he tried to speak, "when he asked you how you got into his truck, you said 'Your mother invited me in.'"

"And then, SLAMMM!" Paul joined in, "He caught you with that blow to the chin. It really rocked your head back. But you didn't seem to feel it. You smiled at Rocky and that pissed him off, so he and Garth Montrose picked you up and threw you over the bed of his truck. You bounced off the hood of a car and hit the ground like a guy skydiving without a parachute. It was great!"

"Oh, it was really nothing," I sullenly said while I tried to recall a trace of events they now reported to me.

"Finally, we picked you up and got Bob Krause to drive you home," Tony said. "And he only agreed to do it if we sat on each side of you and held on to you. So there we were in the back seat. Bob and his girlfriend, and Clint and his honey, were all in the front seat. About a block from your place, you jerk forward and put your hands in front of your mouth and start making all these grunting sounds." Tony looked at Paul who shook his head from side to side with a broad broad smile on his face.

"Go on," I glumly requested.

Taking the cue, Tony proceeded, "So everybody figures you have to royally puke. The girls start screaming; Bob hits the brakes; his car goes skidding; and we get the rear wheels stuck in a snowbank!" After they laughed and exchanged slaps of the hands again, Paul and Tony unraveled more of the story.

Paul added, "Bob didn't care about getting the car stuck as much as he did about getting you out of his car. Everybody wanted you out of the car, and everybody was yelling and screaming and moving fast to get out themselves."

"It was great!" Tony joined in. "We're all falling out of the car, and Paul and me are trying to make sure you get out, and once we have you out, you go off to the side and calmly start unzipping your pants. And as you start peeing, you look up into the sky and say, 'It looks like it's clearing boys.'"

Paul laughed, but managed to control himself enough to explain, "Bob starts yelling at you and asks you what the hell you're doing making him think you're going to puke in his car and then getting his car stuck in a snowbank. Oh, it was great. Everybody else was laughing so hard, except Bob."

"Then what?" I asked indifferently.

"You were really weird, Ricky," Tony replied, and then elaborated, "After Bob finishes yelling at you and he's standing there like you two are going to fight—"

Paul interrupted to ask a clinical question. "You can kick Bob's ass, can't you. Ricky?"

"Yeah, easily," I said with nonchalance as I looked to Tony to continue.

"Well, you zip up your pants and turn around and say, 'Bob, I'd really like to hear more of your sob story, but I have

a big day ahead of me tomorrow,' and you just start heading
up the street to your house." My two companions looked at me
as if they expected an explanation.

Paul said flatly, "You just left. You were still staggering
and you even fell down once, but you just kept walking to
your place. We had to dig the car out and that took about an
hour."

"I'm not sure I want to get drunk with you anymore,
Ricky," Tony said. "Even though some of it was fun to watch."

"Yeah, I don't like to drink the way you do," Paul added.

"Neither do I," I ruefully said as I tried to recall more
about that night.

## 26

They were very concerned about me, and they informed me that I needed help. I listened to my diagnosis and prognosis as my mother and sister explained what they saw as incipient insanity.

"We just really think you need to talk to someone," my sister Mónica began.

"Yes, son," my mother added. "The way you are thinking don't make sense. We are very concerned for you."

I wasn't sure just how I was supposed to act. I admitted to my auditors that yes, indeed I was confused, what with graduation only weeks away and feeling the antithetical tug of being an eighteen-year old kid-adult. But I felt that "talking to someone" was taking the issue farther than was really necessary. Especially when the particular someone they wanted me to talk to was a psychologist, Dr. Howell. The appointment had been set for the following week, and I was to visit with Dr. Howell for as long as it took to make me better.

"Oh, yes," my mother added, "you have to pay for this yourself. We don't have the money to help you with this matter."

"It's a matter that doesn't matter," I grumbled to myself as I stretched out on my bed tossing a football directly above my head and catching it as close to my face as possible without it actually hitting me. My last few weeks of high school— weeks that I had anticipated would be filled with rampant abandonment as far as attending classes was concerned— were greatly checked by my mother's plan to move to the mountains and in with my sister, her husband, and me. Her self-appointed mission was to supervise my graduation and official initiation into the adult world. She wanted to make sure everything went just right, even though I was not excited about attending the graduation ceremony, and was doing so only under extreme psychological duress.

"I don't even know what I did wrong, doctor," I lamented as he studied me. I was sitting in a comfortable, thickly padded chair. My arms were supported by sturdy armrests, the ends of which I clutched with my curled fingers.

"What makes you think you had to do something wrong to visit me?" Dr. Howell asked, his body comfortably positioned in a similar chair, and his persona indicating the work of a scientist.

"Well," I cautiously began, "because the people who come to see you are usually missing a few gears." I felt a little embarrassed at what I had just said, and I offered an expression of inane simpering, kind of like the skinny guy in Laurel and Hardy when he does or says something stupid. After all, here I was, quite possibly one of those with a few missing gears. I wasn't sure that nothing was wrong with me.

"Well, Ricky," the doctor replied, "not everyone who comes here is what you might think they are—crazy. It's just that many people are confused with their lives. Some people find it more difficult than others to cope with themselves and with those around them. They might need a little guidance, or a way of understanding the things that are happening to them, or just someone to talk to who will listen." I wondered how wealthy Dr. Howell was while I nodded my head in understanding. "So why don't you tell me how this whole thing started," he said.

"Well, I have been really depressed lately, and I've been depressed for longer than usual, and I—"

"What do you mean you have been depressed for longer than usual?" Dr. Howell interjected.

I was hesitant to offer such personal information to a stranger in an impersonally sterile-white lab coat, but I explained. "When I usually get depressed, it only lasts for a few days."

"Do you get depressed a lot?"

"Every once in a while. I don't know what a lot is. Just some people have told me it's not good to get that way."

"Who tells you this?"

"Mainly my mother and sister."

"Where's your father?"

"He died."

"How?"

"Suicide," I said. And before he could ask about the method, I added, "with a .38 caliber pistol. He shot himself in the heart."

Dr. Howell looked at me with a subtly intensifying stare. I felt that I may have surprised him about my father and particularly the indifferent, unemotional fashion in which I revealed this information.

"Do you get depressed about your father?" he continued.

"Sometimes, yes," I said in a halting manner. "Sometimes I get really pissed off at him and think he was a big chicken. And other times I think you have to be brave to do something like that."

Dr. Howell slightly tilted and nodded his head and mildly raised his eyebrows to indicate perhaps a logical set of mental premises.

"But none of this is about my dad," I continued. "I was only six years old when he did it, so I really didn't know him."

"So, what do you think this is all about?"

"Okay, well, this is what I see going on." I shifted in my chair and leaned forward a little. "I will be graduating from high school in about a month. My mother and sister think I should go to college because if I go to college I get social security checks every month until I graduate, but only until I'm twenty-five. But I don't want to go to college. In fact I'm not that smart. Even my boss told me all I'm going to do is spend a lot of money moving away to college and in a few months I'll flunk out. And I think I will."

"What would you do if you didn't go to school?" Dr. Howell asked.

"Well, my plans are to travel around the country, especially to the Mississippi River and float down the river like Huck and Jim, except I want to do this by myself. I would like to take Tom, my dog, but he's getting old. I have a lot of money saved up from my work, and if I need more money, I can get a job anywhere. I've been working since I was a little kid." I felt good about what I had just told Dr. Howell, and I looked at him with exigent anticipation. I knew his opinion of what I had just revealed could be the catalyst to the twists and turns my life would take. And in the eyes of my mother and sister, his words would become my existential gospel.

"So, you think I'm crazy, doctor?" I asked pointedly, somehow not caring for the moment.

He laughed a little nervously and shifted in his thick chair before he began. "Ricky, I think you are a normal eighteen-year-old male. What you want to do makes a lot of sense to me, actually. It seems to me that if you decided to go to college, you would be going to school primarily to please your mother and sister, and I think—"

I cut him off for a second as I cynically added, "And to get social security checks."

Dr. Howell chuckled and went on, "What we have here is a decision to be made by you and only you. There will be outside influences, invited or uninvited. There will be all kinds of opinions about your life, some of them emotional ones, some of them psychological, some of them encouraging, even some of them depressing ones. But for you to feel comfortable about yourself, you are going to have to do what you feel is right. The decision you make is not going to sit well with those folks who are a part of your life, but I seriously think you must act with your own conviction. Ricky, do what you want to do, within reason, and listen mostly to yourself. That's all I can help you with. If your mother and sister want to speak with me, I would be more than willing to see them. You do not need to come here anymore."

I thanked the doctor. And as I paid the receptionist, I wondered about the exchange that had just taken place. "Let me see," I thought to myself, "I just paid forty dollars to tell a guy what I want to do with my life, and he said I'm normal, and I go home and tell my mom and sister I'm normal, and everything turns out pretty. I *am* nuts!"

"What did the doctor say?" my mother abruptly asked as she opened the door to my bedroom.

I was changing my clothes, and I could see the shadow of my sister standing behind my mom. "Not much," I hesitantly offered.

"Well, what do you mean not much?" she pressed.

"He just said that I should reconsider the way I feel. That the opportunity to go to college doesn't happen for everybody, and if I go to college now, I could do those other things I want to do later and I'll always have something to fall back on. He said not to worry and that I don't need to go back to see him. He's a nice guy. As I was leaving, he patted me on the back and said, 'Now get those school applications filled out. You're running out of time.'"

I had seen the expectation on my mother's face. We had not maintained a solid relationship over the past few years, and I had rejected all of her ideas, customs, and wishes. On the way home from the doctor's office, I had realized, too, that maybe for my mother, the social security checks had come to represent a link with my father. Even though we knew I was not destined to be a successful college student, we could go through the motions; we could fake it. Symbolically, those checks could show that my long-since deceased father was sending me away to college—and paying for it.

My mother had wanted to be right about this one, and I just couldn't bring myself to tell her that she and my sister were the ones that needed to see Dr. Howell.

# 27

We met in college, at the dorms, through the exchange of supply and demand. He was selling drugs, and I was buying them. In the course of our conversation while striking that initial deal, we discovered that we shared many of the same interests: partying, girls, and sports.

Greg was a pre-law major, and I was one of those first-year students who sign up for a potpourri of classes that demand very little but allow one to officially call himself a full-time college student. It was the first year away from home for Greg, even though his parents lived on the other side of town and were not uncomfortably distant. I was new to the area and had only been on campus a few weeks. The experience of living in a dorm with dozens of other young students was directing my life towards more adventure than I had anticipated.

I held my own at the weekend parties, as my high school had prepared me for such events. My studies, well, they became little hobbies to dabble at while I waited for the next party.

Greg was intense in both school and entertainment. It was vital that he get into a respected law school, at least as far as his parents were concerned. This created much pressure for him, and he found it quite soothing to end most evenings with a little smoke and a little beer. Of course, a core of students who were feeling the same pressures, or at least imagined that we were feeling the same pressures, formed a symposium of young scholars who would pile into a car and drive out to the country and back while we drank, smoked, talked, sang, and got hungry. As the semester progressed, our nighttime country drives became more regular. Some close friendships were developed through the sharing of the bottle and the pipe.

Greg and I became close friends, even though we were not of the same academic or social echelon. I was a bit coarse. I had come from parents who were poor and illiterate, and it was hard to shake that influence. Many times I did not want to hide who I was or where I came from; it felt too phony. So my manner of dress was rustic, and my hair was long enough for a cute little ponytail.

"Let's go over to my parents' house for dinner, Ricky," Greg invited me one night. He threw his dirty laundry on the back seat of his car, and we headed to the lower hills of upper middle-class comfort. We smoked a joint on the way to dinner. My stomach along with my heart and brain told me I was in need of a good home-cooked meal.

I met Greg's parents and tried to be as polite and respectful as possible, knowing that my appearance could be a little shocking to these types of clean folks. I was glad I had showered. Greg toured me through the antiseptic home with its valuable antiques, bright, thick wall-to-wall carpets, and beautifully landscaped gardens.

As we sat down to eat, I noticed the elaborate table setting and became a bit nervous upon discovering that each setting had two forks. I had never eaten with this many implements. I knew I would have to subtly mimic what the others did.

It seemed as if I did everything a half-step behind Greg and his parents. I watched how they cut their meat; where they placed their steak knife once they had made the appropriate cuts; and even how much they salt and peppered, before I aped their motions. I sat up straight, and this made my back hurt. I kept my elbows off the table and ate mostly with my left arm at my side. I took delicate bites and made sure that I chewed my food with the air of an aristocrat.

The conversation developed around Greg's scholastic activities and the types of law schools to which he should apply. His parents were proud that they had worked hard and were able to send Greg to quality institutions. Feeling the effects of what we had smoked on the way to dinner, and struggling with myself to maintain some social decorum, I was glad that Greg was the highlight of the dinner conversation.

A few superficial questions had already been volleyed my way at the start of dinner. The beginnings of self-consciousness appeared when I was asked by Greg's mother what message the length of my hair was attempting to express. I awkwardly answered that I was just following many of the other young students who maintained the same hirsute fashion of the day. Greg's mother exhaled a mildly irritated "hhhmmmppphhh" at this answer, and focused her eyes on the idol who was her youngest child.

"Gregory, you understand that in a court of law, the judge would be making determinations as to your ability if you presented yourself like Rick," she flatly stated, quickly adding for clarity, "I mean his hair, of course." Gregory dutifully responded and promised that he would keep his curly locks to a respectable length.

As I sat eating and listening to how Greg's life would turn out, I felt more and more out of place. I had never had these kinds of confident conversations with my mother. Our communication concerning the future focused on things like *when* I didn't make it in college, what types of jobs I might pursue. Unlike the present conversation I was listening to, when my mother and I discussed college, we knew it was fantasy talk. We had a tacit understanding that I was only attending for ulterior reasons. Teachers, placement tests, and bright students had convinced me by now that I truly was not college material.

I was halfway through my meal when Greg's mother suddenly switched directions in her conversation and looked at me and asked, "Where does your napkin go, Rick?"

I nervously looked over at Greg's napkin-less place setting, then at his father's, and then at my napkin that lay on the table to one side of my plate. I wasn't sure. My first impulse was to tuck the napkin into my shirt, draping it over my chest. I had remembered seeing the Three Stooges do this in a short film called "The Hoi Polloi." But nobody at this table had done this, so I quickly abandoned that idea. I grabbed the linen napkin and without unfolding it, placed it on my right leg. Greg let out a boyish chortle, and his father said something about the Mrs. of the house making sure we all minded our pints and quarts.

I was pretty flushed as the embarrassment lingered for what felt like an eternity. I wanted to tell Greg's mom that I had never sat at a table with linen napkins. I wanted to tell her that in my house we often ate without utensils; we would just tear a couple of pieces of tortilla and scoop food with one piece into the other piece, then pop the filled scoop into our mouths. But there was something about her deportment that told me she would not tolerate such tales. There seemed to be something in her look that assumed that everybody ate with one hand, two forks, crystal glasses, shiny dainty cups, and a cloth napkin.

"You didn't say much at dinner," Greg observed as we got into his car to go home.

"Tired, I guess," I replied.

"Yeah, that was a good meal," Greg said, "and I got my laundry done, too." As the car slowly made its way from the hills to flatland living, Greg offered, "Here, light up a joint, Ricky. We'll stop and get some beer."

From that day on, whenever I have come into contact with linen napkins, I deliberately leave the napkin on the table. I privately dare those dining at the same table to say something about the proper placement of my napkin. I secretly imagine someone asking me where my napkin belongs. And I laugh to myself as I silently respond with "Up your ass!"

# 28

My hand shook violently trying to coordinate a finger with the number I wanted to dial. My head throbbed from my aching hangover. The phone booth no longer had a door, and one of its transparent sides was a starburst of cracked glass. I studied the lines of glass that radiated to a galaxy of hundreds of points bordered by a metal frame, and I thought how it looked more like a spider web. The gray, moody clouds of an early November sky moved slowly overhead, and I pitifully pondered that that was how my brain must look. My palms were slick with sweat as I listened to the impersonal rings, waiting for the phone to be answered.

"Hello?" my mother's sweet and comforting voice called through the telephone receiver.

"Mom? Hi. It's me, Ricky," I timidly began.

"Oh, *m'ijo,* how are you? It's so good to hear your voice."

"Mom, Jennifer left me!" I cried, and I could not say more for a few seconds.

"What? What happen?"

"Jennifer went back home," I sobbed, as a flash flood of acrid water washed down my puffy face and gullied at the corners of my mouth.

"Son, Ricky, are you all right?"

"Do I sound all right to you?" I snapped back as I cried fiercely.

"Now, son, wait. What happen?"

"She just left," I tried again, "and, I know it was my fault, but it still—" I could not finish. My stomach burned and twisted and tried to expel a bile of guilt. I held my right hand over the mouthpiece of the telephone receiver and automatically bent over. My jaws separated as wide as a howler monkey's. My forehead pounded from within, and I straightened up when the storm in my abdomen temporarily subsided.

"Hello? Ricky? Son?" My mother was calling into the receiver when I put it back to my ear again.

"I'm here, Mom," I sadly answered.

"Son, you don't sound so good. What kinds of things have you been doing?"

This question had run through my mind from the day Jennifer had left a week earlier. We had been living together for close to a year, moving into a studio apartment shortly after I was dismissed from college after two semesters. She continued to attend classes while I worked as a warehouseman. But I was immature and bitter. I wanted us to be a handsome college couple, and I had failed in my part of the match. I tried to be how I thought men were with their mates. This translated into abuse in many forms: sexual, emotional, psychological, and spiritual.

I called up an inexperienced reserve of feelings and attempted to convince myself that I was going to be fine one day. "Mom, I know I'll get over this, I guess. But she was the first one and only one I've ever been with." I tried to reassure my mother that I would pull through, but at this moment I needed to talk to someone.

"*Mira, hijito,* it's hard for me. I know how you feel. But because what my life have been like, it's hard for me to help. Yes, you're right, you will be okay. Someone else will come along. But be strong, son. You have to be."

"But I want her to come back!" I cried again.

"Son, I know you two was having problems. That was up to the both of you to work out. I love you very, very much, Ricky, but I'm sorry. Yes, I think it was your fault, too, because I was married to your daddy for too many years, and I raise all you boys. I know what the Coronado mens can be like. But to be honest, son, I wouldn't give two cents for a man's tears."

I pictured myself kneeling down in church as a young boy and thought about all the things that seemed to be my fault. "Okay, Mom, I know. I'm sorry. I'll call next week when I'm feeling better." And I hung up the phone with a weak hand.

The devout young man knelt in church and followed his training as he lightly and repeatedly touched his chest with a clenched fist. "Through my fault, through my fault, through my most grievous fault."

## 29

It really didn't matter to me if I had overdone it. I just didn't seem to care anymore. Having recently flunked out of college created a tremendous rift between most of my family and me. In addition, the only girlfriend I had ever had, left after many months of faithful though not recognized servitude. I was in Lake Tahoe visiting my wild brother—the forgiving and understanding one. He promised that he would help me forget the things that were bothering me, and, if I was interested, he would introduce me to his boss, and I could possibly work in the construction business for a while.

"First things first, Ricky," my brother advised me, lighting a morning joint. "We'll go over to Wayne's house and see what's on the day's agenda, then I want to go check out a Rambler that's for sale."

"Sounds good to me," I hoarsely whispered, attempting to withhold the smoke I had inhaled.

Wayne was my brother's best friend. They worked together, and for them this made work fun. And they kicked off every weekend with a visit to the local casinos to cash checks, have a few drinks, and hospitably welcome the weekend and any female tourists who happened to come with it.

"Hey, Nacho, what's the heavy haps?" Wayne asked my brother as he looked me over. Wayne's hair was greased back with what seemed like a jar of Dixie Peach. His mouth contained gaps where teeth should have been, with an occasional black tooth among the yellow ones that remained.

"Oh, not a whole lot. Just wondering what the gig is today. Wayne, this is my little brother, Ricky."

"Righteous," Wayne answered as he offered me a soiled and calloused hand, then offered us a recreational possibility, "There's a big party over at Dirty Danny's tonight. Actually, Dirty said it starts whenever. We could go over there now and do some partying."

"Sounds like there's some potential there," Nacho replied. "We're going out to breakfast and we came by to see if you wanted to join us."

Wayne decided he would, but first he had something to show us. "Check these babies out," he said as he handed my brother an unlabeled jar of pills.

"Heyyy! Tuinals, nature's pacifiers," Nacho gushed. "Good bedroom drug, too. Where'd you land these?"

Wayne looked a little sheepish at first, only because he knew what my brother's reaction would be. He thought about lying and then confessed, "From Toothless."

Nacho shook his head from side to side. "Wayne, Wayne, Wayne, Wayne. Haven't I told you that doing business with Toothless is risky? I'm kind of disappointed in you. No telling what these things are cut with."

"Yeah, yeah, I know, Nacho," Wayne began, "but him and his old lady were desperate, and I got a good deal for 'em and I plan on making more than my money back at Dirty's. Anyway, I persuaded Toothless that if this is bad shit like the last stuff he burned me with, you and me would go remodel his face."

"What's risky about dealing with this guy?" I innocently asked, trying to be a part of the conversation.

Both Wayne and Nacho looked over at me and seemed surprised at my presence. "Never mind, Ricky," Nacho replied. "You don't want to get involved with these people."

We ate a hearty breakfast at Nacho's and Wayne's favorite place—a combination cafe and laundromat. "This is were the jail gets its food from," Nacho informed me as I looked around at the dingy little cafe. Some of the booths had no tables—only the bolted posts that once supported table tops remained. At our table, the chairs were all different. Nacho sat on a bar stool hunkering over his food like a busy buzzard. Wayne sat in a low secretary's chair with wheels that placed the table top just under his chin. I was hospitably granted a metal folding chair, the kind you find in school auditoriums.

Wayne requested a final cup of coffee, and with it, downed two of the red capsules. "Want some?" he offered.

"Sure," Nacho casually answered, shaking a couple of pills into his palm. Wayne offered the jar to me and I hesitated for a moment at the blatancy of what we were doing.

"Go ahead, Ricky," Nacho urged while he looked around the restaurant. "Nobody's going to tell on us."

I took two of the red pills and finished my orange juice with them. "What do they do?" I asked as we prepared to leave.

"They're like reds," Wayne answered.

"They are reds!" Nacho countered. "And they'll make you kind of drowsy and then belligerent, and then you usually end up fighting and fucking. It's great."

"Sounds like nothing college had to offer," I sardonically quipped, momentarily flashing on the hurts that were making me feel more useless and insecure.

The three of us drove over to see the little square Rambler that Nacho was interested in. "Now is that a sharp short or what?" Nacho asked admiringly as he scanned our faces for concurrence.

"It looks slow," Wayne observed.

"So, who cares about speed?" Nacho responded. "I'm never in a hurry. I'm going to have to seriously think about this one."

As midday approached, we decided to see how active the party was. We pulled into the dirt driveway of a cluttered lot populated by pine trees, motorcycle frames, and old tires. There was a small cabin in the middle of the lot.

"Wayno and NoGo! The Lakeside Loser and The Missing Link!" A large man with wild hair—both on his head and face—yelled out as he stood in the doorway of his hut.

Dirty Danny, or "Dirty," as he was more commonly known, had friendly, sparkly eyes and was the jolly but rough type. He truly lived up to his name as grease and oil seemed to be staples of his domicile. We were invited into his cabin, and we sat in a cluttered living room with centerpieces provided by Harley Davidson. Dirty's baby boy, Harley, sat at his father's feet sucking on a spark plug.

We sat and talked as a joint was passed around. Dirty told us about the beer and wine he had spent a good portion of his paycheck on, and the steaks his wife was bartering for from the butcher who lived across the street.

"The party starts whenever," Dirty explained. He shrugged his shoulders and said, "Hell, it's already started. Can't you tell?"

Wayne offered Dirty a couple of pills, and when he took four at one time, the rest of us popped two more into our mouths. "I got some good sun tea," Wayne informed us. "I made it real strong. It'll go good with these. Won't make us so stupid, you know what I mean?"

The caffeine in the tea countered the drowsy effect of the capsuled drugs, and I was volleyed between feelings and actions of bitter hatred and dreamy complacence. We played darts in Dirty's backyard, and then he slurred a muddy explanation to us about the intricacies and potential of the new carburetor he had just received. We left Dirty's after a few hours and promised him we would be back by nightfall.

"So, what do you want to do now?" Wayne asked.

"I want to see if the people who are selling the car are home," Nacho said.

"Ah, come on, Nacho, forget that car for today. It'll be there tomorrow. Not too many people are in the market for Ramblers." Wayne replied.

"Let's go to the clubs," I blankly suggested.

"Naw, we were there last night," Nacho responded.

"Well, can you drop me off at the clubs and pick me up before you go to Dirty's again?" I asked.

I'm not sure where my brother and Wayne went for the rest of the day or night. Wayne had equipped me with four more of his narcotic candies when they dropped me off in front of a glitzy casino. "Two for you and two for a honey, if you meet one," he said as he shook out my allotment.

I cruised around the casino area for hours. I played a few slot machines and enjoyed a few complimentary drinks. As evening approached, I popped two more barbiturates into my body and slowly staggered outside to catch a breath of fresh air.

I don't remember walking to the liquor store down the street. I do remember paying for a single can of beer and then being accosted by the clerk and some other guys once I stepped outside.

"Excuse me, sir," the clerk asked, attempting to be polite. His two aides stood behind him and to one side. "I have to ask you to show me what's in your pockets," the clerk continued.

"Why?" I asked pointedly.

"Well, to be quite honest with you, sir, we think you shoplifted something while you were in there."

"What?" I calmly but stiffly asked, my attention now fully focused on my accuser's eyes.

"Well," the clerk began, clearing his throat and lightly running his hand over the back of his head, "we're not sure, but—"

I stopped him to belligerently interrupt. "But you're sure I took something?" I held the can of beer inches from his face aiming the opening of the can at his nose and pushed the pop-top up. A mist of beer spitefully sprayed at his face as I expressed a sneering laugh.

The clerk nervously looked to one side in an effort to summon the testimony and reinforcement of his witnesses.

"I'll tell you what," I offered. "I'll let your two shadows inspect all of my pockets." And as I said this, I took a few quick steps backward without looking and into oncoming traffic. Traffic came to a dramatic stop while I stood in the busy boulevard and held my arms straight out from my sides, the beer in one hand.

"Come on," I jokingly invited, "check my pockets."

Horns began to honk and traffic became thick and frustrated. My accuser and his accomplices stood on the sidewalk and dumbly watched me. They did not seem to know what to do.

The patrol car parked in the liquor store parking lot. I remained in the street. A crowd had gathered, and I quickly swallowed the last two pills. The officer stood next to the clerk as they talked.

"Come over here," the officer ordered.

I slowly and deliberately approached the two figures representing commerce and law, alternately shooting looks of crazed hatred at both. Traffic resumed, people cheered, and the cop viciously pulled me by my jacket and pushed me up against the wall. He was incredibly quick with his handcuffs. He jerked me back by my bound hands and walked me to his car. As we approached the car, I broke free and ran back after my accuser who was following us.

My head pounded solidly into the clerk's chest as I ran directly into him like a battering ram. When my head made contact with his heart, I tripped him with my right leg, knocking him down in the parking lot. I kicked him in the ribs a couple of times, calling him a liar and a showoff before the officer and the two shadows jumped on me. I continued to kick and bite anything that felt like flesh until the officer's baton knocked me into a state of shocked docility. I knelt on the parking lot and shook my head, trying to rid my brain of the dull intensifying pain. The officer jabbed me with his baton and told me to lay flat on the ground.

At the police station, my mug shot was taken. While the booking officer fussed with the film, I asked if I could have a set to send to my family. He politely told me to shut up and turn to my left. I was thrown into a cell with another individual who reminded me of one of Nacho's and Wayne's and Dirty's comrades.

"What are you in for?" I slurred.

"Too many tickets," he replied. "How 'bout you?"

I thought for a fuzzy painful moment before answering, "Acting stupid—and getting caught at it."

## 30

It was an early morning phone call, and because of the time, I sensed it was somebody calling with urgent news. My sister was hesitant as she spoke.

"Hello, Ricky?" she said, and then cleared her throat.

"Hi, Mónica, what happened?" I asked, suspecting something was not right and figuring it was about my stepfather.

"It's Ramón. He's had another spell. He's real bad."

"Where *are* you?" I asked, shaking the sleepy confusion from my head.

"I'm at home," she explained, "but Mom called, and she wants us to get over there as soon as possible. I'm going to Richmond to pick Beatrice up, and then we're heading straight to Sacramento. Can you come down?"

"Yeah, I guess so. I'll have to call in and tell them I won't be working today, or tomorrow." And trying to get more information, I asked, "How does it sound? Is this one it, or do you think he'll pull through?" I added for positive effect: "He made it through the first two okay. He might be fine in a few days."

My sister sobbed. She did not say anything for many seconds. "I don't know, Ricky. I think this is it. He's 82 years old. Those attacks take a lot out of him. Even when he's better, he's never as well as he's previously been. He slowly gets worse and worse."

I assured Mónica that I would meet her and Beatrice at my mother's house in a few hours. As soon as I hung up the phone, I got ready to leave, and during the hour and a half trip, I thought about my dying stepfather.

He had been my father figure for over twenty-five years. He had come into my life when I was nine, having first to ask for my mother's hand in marriage before an inquisition held by my four older brothers. I remembered how Andrés had questioned him rigorously and rudely, and how Ramón had successfully defended his intentions with sincere and direct responses. I remembered how he had retired from his job as a warehouseman at a chemical company shortly after marrying my mother. He was immensely proud of his gold watch that three decades of lumping cases and sacks of chemicals had earned him. I remembered those harvest seasons when we worked in the fields together. Despite his age, he could still move quickly and profitably. Later, he asserted his proletarian independence and decided to freelance his labor. We worked as a team of migrant ranch hands traveling throughout the San Joaquin Valley in a pickup truck loaded with tools. We did odd-jobs for farmers and ranchers, often hearing the same teasing joke: "Jacks of all trades, masters of none." We would laugh, even though my stepfather did not fully understand the saying, and I found little humor in it. We worked well together. The only time I got mad at him was when he burned our lunch—burritos scorched to a charcoal blackness by a hot plate we had found in a tool shed we were remodeling. We worked all day without eating; me out of sheer anger, he out of pure guilt.

I thought about how those workdays with my stepfather were valuable to me as he encouragingly taught me how to do many things. He showed me how to hammer a nail with a whip-like stroke of the wrist that conserved energy when there was much hammering to do. He explained the importance of drinking plenty of water during those hot, laborious days. He showed me how to use various power tools, always stressing, "Safety first, *m'ijo.*" He pointed out the financial importance of recycling as we saved barrels of aluminum cans.

I remembered my mother's commandment that Ramón could not lay a hand on me, and if he did, she threatened to light his truck on fire. While she worked afternoons and nights, and my sister Mónica had fled the house for marriage, my stepfather and I were frequently left at home alone to manage things. We employed a system of checks and balances to regulate each other's actions. My mother would administer any reprimands and punishment that she saw fit after receiving daily progress reports. So whenever I did something that broke a house rule, or if I did not finish a chore, Ramón would note it and tell my mother. Whenever he didn't finish a chore, I would tell on him. One day Ramón and I had a serious conversation in which I tried to swing a deal with him. It was a simple offer that if he didn't tell on me, I wouldn't tell on him. But in his wisdom and foresight, he explained to me that telling on each other was built into the system. My mother, an intense woman, expected it. She would want some kind of report when she came home from work, and we couldn't let her down by saying everything was in order. Eventually, Ramón and I became so petty in our criticisms and embellished shortcomings of each other for the sake of having *something* to report, my mother finally abolished the system.

I remembered how my stepfather and I enjoyed watching programs like "Gunsmoke," "The Virginian," and "Bonanza." We were also rabid fans of Show Time Wrestling, and, in his and my mother's bedroom, we sat at the edge of the bed, leaning and yelling into the small television set as we cheered for our heroes until our throats were sore: Pepper Gómez, The Flying Dutchman, and Gentleman James. We moaned with indignation at the ignominious acts of Cyclone Negro, The Sheik, and The Spoiler, who always wore a mask and almost always had it taken off by a good-guy wrestler.

More recent events that redirected my reminiscence included Ramón breaking his wrist and foot when he fell down the stairs in the middle of the night on his way to the kitchen. In his old age, he had developed a habit of making midnight raids on the refrigerator and cupboards, and even if somebody offered to bring a snack or a drink of water up to him, he preferred to do things on his own. After that near-death experience of tumbling down a dark stairway that eventually left him with a permanent limp, my mother purchased a hospital bed with stainless steel rails. This was intended to keep my stepfather in his bed while my mother slept in her own room. But, he soon figured out how to adjust the rails, and with casts on his left wrist and foot, he thump thumped down the stairs to continue his kitchen forays.

My mother grew more concerned with these nighttime trips and sought the help of Ramón's doctor. The doctor offered a dramatic solution, but my mother, who thrived in dramatic situations, was interested. One day while I was visiting, she asked me to help her put my stepfather to bed.

She assertively forced the straightjacket on Ramón as he looked down at the peculiar garment that had extra long sleeves. "Wait," she ordered, as she cinched the buckles in the back while he shrugged and shifted in futile resistance.

"*Oh, no, Querida. ¿Por qué?*" he asked mournfully.

"Because, *Ramoncito del Sol*, you don't listen. You're too *cabezudo*," she scolded. And then she lovingly apologized, "*Viejito,* there's nothing else I can do." She kissed his forehead and then slammed the bed rails up to their highest point.

When we were outside his room, my mother whispered to me that should I stay up late watching television, I was to quietly slip up to my stepfather's room and check on him.

Before turning off the television at about twelve-thirty, I crept upstairs to check on Ramón, who I was sure would be sleeping in the security of his own hugs. I noticed a dim light on in his room, and puzzled, I carefully opened the bedroom door.

He was not in his bed. I rushed to the far corner of his room from where the dull light illuminated quiet activity. Sitting on the floor with scissors in one hand, and working by the light of a small lamp with a bald bulb, Ramón was meticulously cutting the straightjacket into little squares. He looked up at me and, putting an index finger to his lips, whispered, "You *mamá* a crazy lady!"

I arrived at my mother's house before my sisters. The doctor had just left, and a social services' nurse was drawing blood from the crook of Ramón's right arm. I held my stepfather's free hand, and he attempted a weak smile while saying nothing. When my sisters arrived, my mother led us into the kitchen. Her eyes showed traces of crying, but she was now at that empty point when the mind takes a break from the emotions of imminent death. As the nurse tended to Ramón, my mother explained the latest developments.

"The doctor says he is okay," she began. "Ramón doesn't take his medicine like he's supposed to, and they give him a shot and the doctor says he will be fine in a little while. She gulped her last words and slowly offered more. "He wants us to make plans for his funeral."

"Who?" I asked. "The doctor?"

My mother stared at me angrily and said, "Please, Ricky, don't be so *tonto*. Ramón wants us to take care of his funeral, and he wants to know everything. He is very serious."

Beatrice looked confused and said, "What do you mean he wants to know everything?"

Mónica joined the conversation by adding, "He wants us to make all of the arrangements, and then he wants us to tell him about it?"

"Yes!" my mother answered impatiently. "What's so hard to understand? He wants to know what his *caja* will look like, where we are going to bury him, and he said don't worry, he'll take care of what he wants to wear."

"When are we supposed to do this?" I asked.

"Right now!" my mother answered quickly. "He wants to be buried in Richmond. He wants the *misa* to be at St. Marks. He wants the nephews to be pallcarriers because he wants my boys with me in case I pass out."

"It's *pallbearers,* Mom," Beatrice offered with a measured correctness.

"I don't care about that!" she snapped back, and then started crying vigorously.

"Well, where do we start?" Mónica asked. "What do you even call what we're doing? What do we say to the people at the funeral parlor?"

"Don't worry about that, I'll do all the talking," my mother said, quickly regaining temporary composure. "I just want you with me so nobody tries to cheat me. When the nurse's aide gets here, we will leave for Richmond and start making all the plans."

We kissed my stepfather good-bye and promised we would return as soon as possible with all of the details. He thanked us and assured us that he would hang on until we got back.

When we pulled up to the funeral parlor, my sisters and I attempted to inform my mother that we would wait in the car. But she profoundly and profanely urged us, with a stirring speech about death and the plight of the aged, to accompany her inside.

"I want to plan a funeral, but he's not dead yet!" my mother announced as she burst through the doorway of the funeral parlor.

There were three ghostlike women behind the receptionist's desk made up in chalky pastels, wearing subdued and somber dresses. Each woman represented a different generation of female morticians: grandmother, mother, and daughter.

The oldest woman, the grandmother mortician, looked calmly over her bifocals. Her hands were clasped, one resting in the other and held primly in front of her. She politely asked, "Yes, ma'am. You would like to make an appointment for a prearranged funeral?"

"Yes," we answered in unison as the mother mortician gracefully stretched out an arm and directed us into a mahogany-paneled office dominated by a large, orderly, elegant desk. There was a small dish of smelling salts placed towards our side of the desk. Brochures were neatly spread on a credenza. Their titles indicated approaches to death in modern society: *Death as Life, Coping With the Loss of a Loved One,* and *Explaining Death to Your Child.* We sat in puffy chairs. As the eldest mortician stood off to one side with hands eternally joined, the mother mortician began. Her questions were aimed at finding out who, what, and where the intended was. She asked how many children there were. How many guests would be attending, if limousine service would be desired for honored guests, and whether arrangements needed to be made for a reception afterwards.

Mónica carefully whispered in my ear that this was much like planning a wedding. I suggested that both were the same thing. We suppressed nervous giggles as my mother continued to offer more information.

When we had completed the interview, the grandmother mortician unclasped her hands and directed us with a fluid motion of her arms into an adjoining room. We entered a large, beautiful showroom with the latest coffin models tastefully displayed. Beatrice and Mónica ooohed and aaahed, and my mother said, "What pretty furniture!"

We stared for minutes at the various coffins while the two morticians stood ethereally to one side with their hands clasped and their faces adorned with heavenly smiles waiting for us to choose. My sisters began to cry, my mother awkwardly attempted to comfort them, and the mortician ladies were professionally cognizant enough to exit the showroom and leave us to perform our dubious task in privacy.

"How do we choose?" Beatrice whispered as if we were in church.

"I don't know," my mother whispered back.

We summoned one of the morticians in to shed some light on the process of choosing a casket. The mother mortician

informed us that people bury their loved ones in something
that reminds them of the deceased. She pointed to a majestic
redwood casket and said, "One young man buried in a casket
like this one was a carpenter. He loved to work with wood. He
died in a tragic accident. This is the model his parents chose."
She showed us a casket with distinct antique brass handles.
This model, she said, had been reserved for a woman who
loved and collected antiques.

My mother pointed to a casket lined in a shimmering and
glowing blue. "This is pretty. What do you call this?" she
asked.

"Oh, that's a very smart model," replied the mortician.
"That's called Air Force Blue. It is stunning with an American
flag draped over the deceased. Was your husband in the military?" she asked.

"No," my mother answered. "He was from Mexico."

"He did love this country though," I pointed out. My
mother, my sisters, and the mortician looked at me curiously.
"Well, he did. He was very patriotic. He voted in every elec-
tion he could. And he could even recite the Preamble to the
Constitution," I stressed, defending myself.

They thought for a few moments, and finally my mother
said, "Let's get this one. This would be a very good one for
Ramón. I know he will like it."

We returned to the mahogany office, consummated the
final preparations and fulfilled the financial obligations. The
more maternal mortician complimented us on our choice and
informed us that Ramón's name would appear on various
funereal accoutrements.

When we got back into the car, we released a collective
sigh. "Boy, that was stressful," Beatrice said.

"Yeah, it was," I agreed.

"And sort of spooky, too," Mónica added.

We giggled tentatively until my mother said, "Stop playing around. We got to go to the cemetery." And we prepared
for our next stop.

Before we went into the office at the cemetery, we agreed
that my mom would not do too much of the talking. Mónica
volunteered to negotiate this one, and once inside, she quickly
concerted the purchase of a double plot.

The cemetery real-estate agent gave us the particulars of
what we were purchasing: "It's nine-hundred dollars for two

plots, one burial; fourteen-hundred dollars for two plots, two burials."

"Why does it cost so much more for the second one?" my mother asked.

The explanation was that it cost five-hundred dollars to open the ground after the first burial.

"Well, I'm not going with him just to save five-hundred dollars," my mother joked as she began to loosen up. She then asked with personal concern, "What happens when my husband dies first and then I die later. Who will pay to bury me?"

"Certainly, your children would cover that cost, Mrs. Del Sol," the salesman answered, scanning our faces for approval.

"Go for the package deal, Mom!" Mónica offered.

"Yeah, get it while it's on sale, Mom," I added.

Beatrice chimed in, "We might not have five-hundred dollars, Mom; we like to go to Reno a lot." And we laughed as the salesman shifted his eyebrows questioningly and invited us to choose the plots.

Influenced by the meaningful symbolic connections we had learned from the morticians, we chose two spaces that were tucked at the back of one section of the cemetery. Directly behind these plots was a full and nicely tended flower garden. There was a solitary young tree to one side of and a few feet away from Ramón's and my mom's burial sites. We rationalized that Ramón had always loved working in his garden, and we decided that he would be buried in the space that was closest to the tree. Satisfied, we had the salesman draw up the final papers; my mother signed her name on appropriate lines; and we headed for home.

We excitedly ran up to Ramón's bedroom. The nurse's aide informed us that he had had a very good day. He ate quite a bit during supper, and he was much more attentive and alert than he had previously been. We sat him up in his bed, placed plump pillows behind him, and told him all about the day's events. His eyes glimmered with joy as he asked many questions. We talked at length about his funeral and told him about the significance of the casket we had picked out and the location of the plot he would be buried in. He then told us he had a surprise.

He dismissed my mother and sisters and asked me to stay behind to help. He pointed to his closet, and with my assistance, he put on some sharply creased black slacks, dark dress socks, shiny black shoes, a crisp white shirt, and a blazing blue tie. I reached for his suit coat, but he rejected that and motioned to a white box sitting on a shelf in his closet. He was as excited as a young bride. I carefully opened the box. Inside was a brand new Los Angeles Dodgers team jacket.

I helped him with the jacket and he said, "*Ya*, let's go show your *mamá*." He walked slowly out into the hallway, and, calling downstairs for my mother and sisters, he stood at the top of the stairs with his arms stiffly spread in a mannequin-like pose modeling his outfit. He smiled and said, "This is what I wearing to my funeral."

My mother rushed up the stairs followed closely by my sisters. They were more concerned with him being out of bed and standing on his own than they were with what he was wearing. When they finally focused on his funeral attire, my mother asked, "You want to wear *that* to your funeral?" Mónica counseled Ramón that all of his friends and family would be there and that he might look better if he wore his suit coat rather than the bright blue Dodger jacket.

"*Este es mi último deseo.* It's my funeral," he declared as he slowly limped back into his room.

We all looked at each other, and finally Beatrice said with a pleading seriousness as she followed him into his room, "But *Ramón, por favor,* the people who will be at your funeral are mostly San Francisco Giants fans."

## 31

*Una de las cosas que más recuerdo de mi padrastro es que él siempre era muy chistoso. Por ejemplo, una vez después de misa cuando mi mamá le presentó a la monja Josefina a mi padrastro, él la recibió a ella con la pregunta divina: "¿Y dónde está José corriente?"*

*Otra vez cuando un hombre le preguntó a mi padrastro si él era casado, respondió, "¡Claro que sí, y casado por las tres leyes!"*

*El hombre, parecía confundido y le preguntó a mi padrastro, "¿Cuáles son las tres leyes del matrimonio? ¿El Padre, el Hijo y el Espíritu Santo?"*

*"N'ombre," contestó mi padrastro, "las tres leyes del matrimonio son la ley civil, la de la iglesia, —¡y la del pendejo!"*

*Mi padrastro también tenía un cuentito de cuando se casó con mi mamá. "Bueno", comenzaba, "tu mamá y yo estábamos hablando, y yo le pregunté si quería 'cazar' conmigo. Ella me abrazó y con felicidad gritó, '¡Ayyy Ramoncito del Sol, sí, sí, sí, me quiero casar contigo!' Y al siguiente día, nos casamos en una iglesia. Pero yo creí que íbamos a 'cazar' en un campo." Y, con ese cuentito, mi padrastro me dejó con un consejo: "Hijito, antes que te cases, mira lo que haces".*

*Me reía mucho con mi padrastro. La primera vez que mi mamá le puso el apodo a mi padrastro de "ojos de chino", él decía, "¿Y sabes qué, viejita? Parece que soy chino, pero hablo japonés. ¿Sabes cómo decir 'dedo' en japonés? ¡Sacamocos!"*

*Y mi padrastro fue chistoso hasta el final. Cuando se estaba muriendo, mi mamá me mandó a la recámara de mi padrastro para quitar de una de las paredes un retrato de* Marilyn Monroe *porque el sacerdote venía para darle la última bendición.*

*Antes que me llevara el retrato, mi padrastro me pidió un favor, "Ricardito, por favor, déjame ver el retrato de* Marilyn Monroe *una vez más antes de morir." Y yo, muy triste y con la*

*cara mojada de llanto, le presenté el retrato a mi débil padras-*
*tro. Y con eso él dijo en un grito final, "¡Ayyy, qué curvas, y yo*
*sin frenos!"*
   *Y nos reímos una última vez.*

===============

One of the things I remember most of about my stepfather was his sense of humor. For example, one day after mass
when my mother introduced Sister Josephine to him (in Spanish Jose [Joseph] fina [fine]), my stepfather welcomed her
with the question "and where is José Corriente (Ordinary
Joseph)?"

Another time a man asked him if he was married. "Of
course!" he answered, "and married by three different laws!"

Puzzled, the man asked my stepfather, "What are the
three laws of marriage? The Father, the Son and the Holy
Spirit?"

"No, sir," my stepfather answered. "The three laws that
apply to marriage are civil law, church law, and the fool's
law!"

My stepfather also had a story about the time he married
my mother. "Well," he began, "your mother and I were talking
and I asked her if she wanted to go hunting *(cazar)* with me.
She hugged me and joyfully screamed, 'Ooh, Ramoncito del
Sol, yes, yes, yes, I want to marry *(casar)* you! And on the following day we got married *(casar)* in a church. But all the
time I thought we were going hunting *(cazar)* in the country."
So, my stepfather would add this advice. "Before you get married, son, make sure you know what you are doing!"

I used to laugh a lot with my stepfather. The first time
my mother gave him the nickname "Chinese eyes," he said,
"You know what, old lady? I look Chinese, but I speak Japanese. Do you know how to say finger in Japanese? SACAMO-
COS! (booger picker)."

And my stepfather kept his sense of humor to the end.
When he was dying, my mother sent me to his room to
remove a picture of Marilyn Monroe he had on the wall before
the priest arrived to give him the last blessing.

Before I took away the picture, my stepfather asked me
for a favor. "Ricky, please let me look at Marilyn Monroe's pic-

ture once more before I die." And I, with great sadness, presented the picture to my then very weak stepfather. And at this he gave one last cry, "Ohh, what curves, and me without breaks!"

And we laughed together one last time.

## 32

"My God! What happened?" my wife asked as I slowly entered the house crying.

"Nothing," I sobbed.

"Ricky, Honey," she tried again, "What's wrong?" She stood in front of me, not allowing me to pass to the comfort of my bed where I planned to cry until I left for work that afternoon. "Honey, what happened? Please, Ricky," she pried.

"It's just school again," I said as I tried to regain some composure, "and fucking teachers!"

She led me to the couch. "Here, Honey, sit down," my wife offered. "Lunch will be ready in a few minutes. If you want, we can talk about what happened."

I looked at my wife, who looked back at me with sympathy. I thought about how strong she was. She could take so much. And in our young married life and the careful courtship before that, I had never seen her break down the way I did; she rarely cried. And when she did cry, it was usually for an animal. Mark Twain was right, training really is everything.

While the soup simmered, we sat on the couch and I told my miserable story.

"I was in the writing lab. You know, the one I'm taking just to pick up a couple of extra units. And since it is largely made up of independent-study students, we are all on our own. We do have to produce ten pages of writing a week, but that's no problem, because there's always the neighbors to write about."

I had settled down by now, and I related the events of the morning as the tears dried on my face, causing a light tightening of my skin. "So I have all my writing done and I'm feeling good about myself because the instructor is always going around ragging on people for not doing their work. But I'm different, right? You know, I'm at least twelve years older than most of the students in the class, so naturally I've learned by now to get my work done." I added for persuasive effect, "We re-entries are that way."

"Anyway," I continued, "I'm reading a grammar book and really enjoying my simple little existence. I'm feeling productive and resourceful because I figure if I want to be an English teacher, I'd better know this stuff inside and out. There was an explanation of intransitive verbs that I didn't understand. So what am I naturally going to do?"

"Ask the instructor, of course," my wife answered with a tone of confident rationality as she carefully placed the steaming bowl of soup on the coffee table.

"Fuck the instructor, of course!" I answered as anger resurfaced for a vicious verbal blow. "Yeah, okay, so I do that. I raise my stupid insignificant hand, and when she comes up to me, I ask her if she can explain this bullshit about in-fuck-ing-transitive verbs. Not in that manner, of course, and not with those words. You know me, Honey, I'm a polite guy, and heretofore, I had the utmost respect for all instructors."

My wife enthusiastically nodded her head to affirm that yes indeed, I was a decent person.

I went on, "So she takes the book and reads to herself for a few studious moments and then says, 'This book is too sophisticated for you,' and then she puts it back on the bookshelf! Can you believe that shit?"

My wife shook her head rapidly from side to side as if someone had surprisingly punched her.

"What?" she exclaimed, looking perplexed as I bobbed my head while staring at her.

"Yeah," I recounted, "she just took the book, said what she said, put it on the shelf, I come home crying and feeling useless, end of story. What's real interesting is, I paid for this crap!"

"Well, what did you do? What did you say?" my wife inquired as the ire rose to her face.

"Nothing. I just sat there embarrassed and feeling like I didn't belong. I figured she was right. After all, she's the instructor. I'm just a stupid, artless, factory worker who has been on the assembly line for the past ten years trying to enter an unfamiliar world. I even make it a point to not let my blue-collar influence elbow its way into my learning. I'm counting on the fact that she is professionally trained, which means, she knows and I don't. Although, I know if I ever became a teacher, I would never say something like that to anybody. Does part of being a teacher include being rude and insensitive?" And as I asked this, I choked on the emotions that barometrically rushed in and caused torrents to flow down my face.

My wife was not really listening to me at this point. Her mind was processing many of life's variables and conditions that to her knowledge and experience made people react to things the way they do.

"She didn't know," my wife calmly stated.

"What?" I asked, as I blew on my soup to cool it.

"She couldn't explain intransitive verbs to you, Honey. She didn't know about them herself," my wife theorized, assuming the demeanor of a detective who solves a murder.

"She didn't know?" I asked dubiously. "Oh, come on. You're just sticking up for her."

"No, no, Honey," she urged. "I believe she really did not know and was too proud or something like that to admit it." She continued, "Granted she should not have responded the way she did, but I would not let that reflect on you or your abilities. You've been in school for a year now. You're a full-time student, and you work full-time, and you're making the dean's list. How many more class meetings do you have with this suppressing person?"

"Too many," I replied. "There are still five more weeks left in the semester."

"Well," she attempted, "don't let one instructor get to you like that, Honey. Next time ask how you can relieve that lack of sophistication. Say, 'Will you teach me to be more sophisticated?' Make them answer to something. They don't know everything. They want to make you think they do, but they don't. It's just that people, even seemingly educated and enlightened people, have a very difficult time admitting to their shortcomings. Ego is a big deal."

I leaned over and nestled my head in my wife's lap. "It's just that it hurts so much, Honey. Why does education have to be like this? All my life I have wanted to be like one of those instructors, and all my life I have been made to feel inadequate by them. And they call this the Humanities. It should be called the *in-humanities*, or the *sub-humanities*."

I began to cry again softly. My wife slowly ran her fingers through my hair and caressed my wet face.

"It'll be okay, Honey," she soothed, "Why don't you take a nap, and I'll wake you up when it's time to get ready for work. Someday we'll be done with this craziness we call life."

"I know, Honey," I apologized. "I just wish it would hurry."

## 33

I'm a new Mexican. And I owe it all to my education. When I started going to college only a few months after my thirtieth birthday, I knew I wanted to be a teacher. I had been a factory worker for too many years, and nothing interesting or exciting was happening in my life. With a goal firmly set, I focused on the journey ahead of me. School was an experience of many surprises.

After graduating from junior college, I attended a small private college and graduated with a degree in Humanities. I continued with more upper-division courses at a state university, working toward a Master's degree in English. It was there that I slowly became a new Mexican.

As counselors advised me on what courses to take, they also encouraged me to apply for minority grants and scholarships. I did this with some hesitation. For some reason, I felt guilty about receiving money for being a member of a minority group. But, I applied for everything that was ethnically available and received most of what I had applied for.

As I entered graduate school, advisors urged me to capitalize on anything being offered to minority students. It was explained to me that there was a tremendous need for minority faculty at schools and universities; that Affirmative Action was there for me, and that I should not let opportunities pass me by. A strange term, I had thought. Affirmative, a form of the word *affirm*. A word derived from Latin and meaning "to strengthen, make strong." And combined with the word *action* to indicate the process of activity or doing. Again, I applied for grants and fellowships, and again I received that which I had flinchingly sought.

On one occasion my picture made it into the university newspaper, along with other "students-of-color" who had also been awarded sizable fellowships. I had balked at applying for the fellowship, telling encouraging professors that I felt funny about the whole thing. "They seem like genetic scholarships," I explained. But I was persuaded, and by this time, I had quit my factory job, so I was mildly desperate.

A colleague greeted me one morning and congratulated me on my fellowship endowment. I humbly thanked him, and for some reason, I felt I should explain to him that it was merely for having the right genes at the right point in history. What I had been awarded had very little to do with actual talent, I added.

He cleared his throat and expressed his true feelings and his anger at seeing, "all these minorities getting money just for being minorities." He frustratingly told me how unfair school was, and how white people were getting shafted. And then he ripped into my existence with a final "And you don't even *look* Mexican!"

My face grew warm with embarrassment. I apologized to him for the way things were and tried to explain that I would have been a fool not to apply for such an offering. "The programs are there and professors kept telling me to apply," I said, trying to blame others for my good fortune.

We parted, and as I walked to the financial-aid office to pick up another academic welfare check, I thought about how the whole system seemed biblical in an Old Testament sort of way. I mean, it seemed that a generation of younger whites were cursed for the machinations and institutions devised and implemented by generations of older whites.

As I stood in line for my check, my thoughts turned to my illiterate parents who had struggled for many years, working in the fields and packing houses, and who didn't seem to have the opportunities that others unlike them had. I thought about my own indoctrination into the work force as we picked, packed, and pruned various crops for powerful white landowners from the Santa Clara Valley to the San Joaquin Valley.

I thought about that other language that ran through my head and tugged at my essence whenever I heard the spirited songs and crystal-sounding strumming of guitars, violins, and harps. I thought about the rich smell of different looking foods that always left me feeling full and comfortable. And I thought about how at one time I had tried to deny all of this. I tried not to be Mexican. Not to speak a Mexican's language and sing Mexican songs. Not to eat Mexican food.

As I walked to my next class, I respectfully thanked my education for not allowing me to forget my good fortune of being a proud, hard-working Mexican. A Mexican who speaks, sings, eats, loves, feels, and reacts with a sensibility of something different, something special, something alive and awakening. *"¡Soy mexicano por fortuna!"* I said to myself as I recalled a humble song and sat among a class of white faces.

## 34

"Ricky Coronado," the announcer's voice declared.

"Not bad for a *gabacho*," I said to myself as I noticed the authentic accent with which the announcer pronounced my last name at the graduation ceremony. "I don't even pronounce my name that way," I mused. "I've anglicized it. That's what I get for being a Northern California Mexican."

I felt quite lonely the day I was to graduate with my Master's degree in English. My wife and her mother were with me, but I missed the hugging, joking, and laughing of my own family. I missed my mother's flour tortillas; I missed the Mexican music; I missed the closeness of family members packed around the dinner table playing cards. Graduating was anticlimactic. Why did it have to be this way? I recalled my educational journey.

It started when I suddenly found myself frustrated and unhappy with my life. I was thirty years old when I decided to go back to school. I had devoted many years working full-time at an electronics company as an assembly-line worker. I knew that I didn't want to be soldering little cable wires to printed circuit boards for the remainder of my unremarkable life. There were opportunities to compete for middle-management positions. But the corporate realm and corporate language seemed to be marked by deception. And I had convinced myself that to be a manager of labor, meant usually to be a liar to labor. At this point, it was only to myself that I could be untrue.

I visited a counselor at the local junior college. We talked about the things that interested me. I told him that I was fully bilingual and had an affinity for language and literature, but that I really didn't know what I wanted to do. "I think I want to be a teacher, an English teacher, but I'm not sure if I'm smart enough."

I started school cautiously. A vivid, painful memory of flunking out of the same junior college eleven years before lingered in my mind. I was determined not to repeat my immature actions. I worked swing shift at the factory and went to school during the day.

The first semester I took three classes. I did not talk about my education to my family; they were busy pursuing or enjoying the products of success. I did not tell my mother I had reentered school because she was quite cynical and did not have much respect for book readers. I wanted to tell some of my nephews and nieces who were also college students, but they seemed to exude a demeanor of blasé refinement when I asked them about their own college experiences.

I floated alone on the elixir of learning. A world of knowledge was presented to me, and I tried to consume the essence of each subject as I learned how the world worked.

I graduated from the junior college and enrolled in an alternative private college which allowed me to attend classes on weekends rather than during the week. I was still a factory worker, but I felt better about myself because it seemed that for the first time in my life, I was successful at something meaningful.

As my education captured most of my attention, my relationship with my family weakened. Maybe there was just no time. I do know that my thinking changed—it had to if I was to survive in college.

I became what academia calls "a critical thinker." I had even taken a required class that taught me how to do this. I learned to analyze what people say and write, and to recognize various types of arguments and appeals. I discovered that I no longer had the same outlook toward things the way most of my family still did.

God was the first to go, or rather, religion. And I think that my growing critical awareness, which seemed to be oddly characterized with my mother's cynicism, inadvertently ripped into the very ethos of my own family.

"This is my son-in-law," my mother-in-law gushed to the unsuspecting waiter. "He just graduated with a Master's Degree in English."

Both my wife and my mother-in-law were quite pleased and proud of what I had achieved and how I had done it. They had been immovable stanchions of support during my tense college and blue-collar period. I, however, felt none of their enthusiasm. The future did not look so bright to me, only more intimidating. My intellectually maturing mind was also growing gradually polluted with a miasmic maelstrom of frustration, confusion, defeat, and loss.

I never bothered to tell my mom that I was in school. She would not understand, and by now, we only spoke to each other a few times a year, even though she lived only ninety miles away. In fact, I had not spoken with a single member of my family during my last five years of college. My wife maintained a close friendship with one of my sisters, and it was through this relationship that I received news bytes about the rest of my family.

Soon after my graduation, as I was learning that the job market for a Master of English with limited practical experience was not very promising, my wife suggested that perhaps it was time to break the silence and tell my mother about me.

"It'll make you feel better about yourself, Honey," she said. "You've been saying that you want your mother to be proud of you and that you'd really like to surprise her."

I thought about it for a minute. I thought about how surprised and proud my mother could be. All I had been to her for most of my life was a worker, albeit a good one. To suddenly tell her that I no longer worked in a factory, that I was an English teacher and had even taught my own classes during my last year of graduate school, could be quite a thrill for her. "Good idea, Honey," I said to my soulmate. "I'll call her and tell her I want to visit for a day or two."

When I talked to my mom on the phone, I did not tell her about my new life; I wanted to surprise her. The next day I drove to her house in Sacramento. I was nervous as I pulled into the driveway. I had flowers in one hand and a thin file folder in the other hand.

My mother opened the door, and we hugged with the embrace of long lost relatives now found. She wiped tears from her eyes as she lovingly placed the flowers in a vase.

"Oh, it's so good to see you, *m'ijo*," she cried as she held my hand. "Why do you stay away from us? What did we do to you?"

I cleared my throat before explaining anything. "I have something to tell you, Mom."

"Oh, no, *no me digas. Te vas a morir,*" she gloomily guessed.

"No. No, Mom, I'm not going to die."

She smiled and patted my hand., "Tell me, what's going on in your life?"

I reached for my file folder and pulled out a piece of official looking paper. "Read this," I offered, knowing that she would only be able to read some of the letter and understand even less. "I'll help you. We'll only read the first part." We read slowly:

Dear Mr. Coronado:

On behalf of President Hansen, I am pleased to offer you an appointment as a Teaching Associate at Sonoma State University for the 1991-92 school year in the Department of English.

She looked closely at the letter, examining the letterhead, checking the date, and rereading the person's name to whom the letter was addressed.

"What does this means?" she asked as she looked me up and down.

"Let's read the last part," I suggested. And we focused our attention on the concluding paragraph:

We look forward to your joining our teaching staff and trust that your association with us will be professionally rewarding. To acknowledge your acceptance of this appointment, please sign the enclosed duplicate copy and return it to my office as soon as possible.

Thank you.

The letter was signed by a Dean of Academic Affairs. I looked at my mother as I released a widening smile.

She was still confused and cleared her throat a little before she began, "Who are they talking about? *You?*"

"Yes!" I beamed, "I don't work in the factory anymore. I'm a college English teacher and I just finished teaching my own classes at Sonoma State, you know where that is." Before I could explain what I had been doing with my life during the past years, my mother suddenly recollected of where I was talking about.

"Oh, yes! I know that place," she said, "That's where your nephew Manuel, he wrassles. He was the champion. Do you see him there? Oh, he's something, that boy." And she began to relate the illustrious wrestling career of my nephew to me.

I realized that in the eyes of my mother, being an English teacher couldn't hold up to being a champion high school wrestler. I suppressed the anger that was exploding within me and the tears that were gathering from the sensations that my brain was producing. My mother continued, now delivering the biography of another one of my talented nephews, this one a promising baseball player.

I decided not to fight it and asked how the rest of the family was doing, even though I didn't really care. As I asked superficial questions about people I didn't want to know about, I planned my escape.

After a hasty dinner at a restaurant, we returned to my mother's house. I decided to drive back to my own home rather than spend the night. I made a fake phone call and fabricated an emergency professional meeting. I made up a pretentious excuse that an important meeting had suddenly been arranged—how fortunate it was that I had phoned a colleague—and it was imperative that I attend early the next day. I explained to my mother that it would be best if I drove home that night.

I cried all the way home. I thought about what my diploma had read and considered the worth of what I had put myself through. I thought about many of my peers who were already applying to Ph.D. programs. I thought about the jobs that were not there and the economy that scarcely was.

A few days after my graduation, my wife had proudly given a copy of my thesis to my sister. I had enjoyed working on my thesis. After years of reading the English literature of men like Chaucer, Shakespeare, Milton, Swift, the Romantic Poets, Arnold, and Joyce; and after absorbing the American literature of men like Paine, Thoreau, Melville, Twain, O'Neill, Steinbeck, and Carver, I had stumbled upon the works of talented Mexican-American writers. I was surprised to find that there was such a thing as Chicano literature, and that Chicanos were writing. And from this literature, I was touched with memories of my family; it was the language.

And it was that bilingual, bicultural, and lyrical language that I chose to address in a very general thesis.

My sister, who had dabbled at college throughout her twenties, thirties, and forties, read my thesis, and in the spirit of scholarship, wrote a few notes. Shortly after my graduation, my wife handed me my thesis with my sister's comments clipped to the front. I sat on the couch late one night and excitedly began to read my sister's comments. I was interested because a few years had passed since we had spoken to each other, and at one time, we had been very close.

The comments were superficial and basic. Her peroration took on a different tone though. She concluded her analysis with a very disturbing:

> There is a problem with educating *La Raza*. I can't help but think the things you've learned and the things you've written do nothing more than produce a fabricated Mexican.

I read this little piece of social science with confusion. "What's a fabricated Mexican?" I asked myself. "And what would an unfabricated Mexican be?" I thought about the times we picked plums and grapes. "I'll bet that's what she means by a *fabricated Mexican*. If you're not working physically hard and you're Mexican, I guess some would see that as less authentic, made-up, out of the environment in which God gave us to work—the fields—and with shorter bodies to fit into those trees and vines. I suppose it could even be considered anachronistic to some," I hypothesized. "But everybody's fabricated. And for *La Raza* the time is now," I said to the turned off television as I looked at my own form on the black screen and wondered who I really was and what I had become. There was irony in my education as it had changed me, maybe even improved me; but it also separated me from family, language, and culture, making me a stranger to those with whom I had once been familiar.

I thought for a few quiet minutes before I concluded, "Anyway, we all wear social masks to fit certain situations. I am definitely a fabricated Mexican. I'm also a fabricated student. Husband. Son-in-law. Teacher, now. A guy who drinks beer and watches football with a few other guys on Sunday.

I'm all of these people, and it's language that allows me to be them."

"Besides," I began lecturing to the dog who was beginning to lightly snore, "it's not a problem educating anybody."

## 35

After years of self-abuse through alcohol and drugs, I could not stand it any longer. I had to know what happened, and there was nobody to ask who would give me a straight answer. I decided to do what my college education had taught me. I researched my father's death. I had always known how my father had died, but I was looking for concrete details. I was looking for evidence that would indicate that even though I came from him, I would not end up like him. I wanted to live. I wanted that silent persistence that my stepfather had tried to pass on to me. That persistence that showed that the motion of life is a dialectic process, and you move, shift, and make adjustments within the paradox the best you could.

The mail arrived. I looked at the official envelope with the return address of the Contra Costa County Sheriff-Coroner's office. An anxious curiosity consumed me. I would have the next few days to absorb this information alone since my wife was away on business. And I had only twenty minutes to get to class. For a moment, I deliberated whether to grab my keys and leave, or read the contents of the thick envelope. I ripped the envelope open. Inside was the reality of my father's death.

I hastily read the autopsy report, which was largely medical and technical jargon. There was also a Deputy Coroner's Preliminary Report, a Supplemental Report, and a Certificate of Death.

When I got home from school that night, I turned on a dull light and sat on one end of the couch. I started with the autopsy again, thinking that I would get the most objective report from that bit of information. The report was divided into two main sections. The first section described the "External Examination," and the rubric that introduced that narrative, read: Marks of Identification:

The body was that of a rather small, partly bald middle-aged male. There was an 8cm. laceration longitudinally along the dorsum of the right wrist. There was a small round penetrating wound over the left 4th interspace 5cm. to the left of the mid-line. This measured 8mm. in diameter and its edges were inverted. There was a small grayish area of abrasion at the wound margin. This was definitely a wound of entrance. No powder burns were noted, but if the subject had been clothed these would not have shown on the body. Another wound, obviously a wound of exit, was noted on the posterior aspect of the left chest directly inferior to the interior angle of the scapula. Considerable amount of post mortem abrasion was noted on the anterior thighs and the anterior abdomen and chest evidently due to action of insects, probably ants, a few which were still noted on the body. Livor mortis was mainly anterior and rigor was essentially gone.

I continued with the next section of the report, the "Internal Examination." Its heading read: Thoracic Cavity. Before plunging into that descriptive essay, I held the report in my left hand, my arm draped over the armrest of the couch. I did not want my tears to ruin the report, and sometime later, when my weeping body settled down, I continued reading:

The left pleural cavity contained in excess of 2 liters of blood. The penetrating wound had passed through the 4th left interspace and thence into the pericardium. It passed completely through the left ventricle of the heart and produced the massive hemorrhage noted. The projectile then passed through the lower lobe of the left lung and left the left thoracic cavity through the 10th rib about 7cm. to the left of the mid-line. During its course it passed slightly laterally and 10 to 15 degrees interiorly. There was about 100cc. of blood clot in the pericardial cavity and a small amount of blood clot in the right pleural cavity. The heart vessels and valves were normal. The lungs were normal except for much blood in the alveoli of the left lower lobe and in the main bronchial tree.

A concluding paragraph of two sentences read:

There was an odor resembling alcohol about the body cavities. With a pistol, the wound could well have been self-inflicted.

I slowly rose from the couch and went into the kitchen. The shot of tequila went down effortlessly. The second shot fueled the flame in my mind as it burned inside my body. I popped open a beer and with a trembling hand pushed a José Alfredo Jiménez tape into the cassette player. He was my father's favorite singer. I returned to the corner of the couch as the lyrics of "La Enorme Distancia" began. I sat for a while and listened to the rest of the cassette, the other songs moaning the recurring motifs of death and the worthlessness of life.

"He was drunk when he did it," I thought. "I wonder if his last drinking session was carried out with a sense of private ceremony? Maybe it was intended as a sedative before the operation. Do you suppose he died immediately, or did he have time to writhe, and moan, and regret?"

I pointed my right index finger with my thumb up, my hand resembling a gun. With the information I had just swallowed, I put my hand up to my chest trying to copy the angle of the gun, imagining how the bullet had traveled through the heart and lung, finally exiting the body.

The sweat from my forehead met the tears from my eyes, and my breathing became heavy and staggered. My chest tightened as if an enormous weight had been placed on it.

My thoughts were now rampant as José Alfredo sang a bewailing song: "No vale nada la vida, la vida no vale nada. Comienza siempre llorando, y así llorando se acaba...." I reflected on the sadness of the lyrics: "Life is worth nothing, there is no value to life. It always begins with crying, and with crying it also ends...." I turned the music louder and privately dared the grease monkey in the apartment next door to complain about it. I wondered what kind of grade the coroner got in English composition. I asked the air if it took courage for my father to do it. And I thought about the gun he used. It had a holster with a horse's head stitched on it. It was in my closet. It was the only thing of my father's that my mother had given me. Why couldn't I have inherited a baseball mitt, or a fishing pole, or a watch?

I went through the other papers and read the police report. Under the heading of crime "Suspicious Circumstances" was typed. I bitterly laughed and said, "Life is a suspicious circumstance."

Under the heading of suspect, the information read:

Coronado, Ignacio. 5'6" 155 lbs. Brn eyes Blk hair, graying Gray felt hat and new brown shoes. Speaks very little English.

The next section of the report instructed the reporting officer to: 1. Reconstruct the crime. 2. Describe physical evidence and location found; give disposition if not booked. 3. Summarize other details relating to the crime. 4. Itemize and describe property.

"Well, let's see how closely Philip Marlowe followed the assignment," I muttered cynically:

Mrs. Coronado had gone to pick up the children at school and upon her return found on the bed, the open holster and ten rounds of .38 cal. Ammo, weapon gone. Talked with Mr. Garza he stated that Mr. Coronado had left a half hour prior approx. 2:45 P.M. walking West on Sutter.

I remembered the Garzas. They were older, and all of their children had moved away. Mrs. Garza used to baby-sit with me every once in a while. She was very grandmotherly. I continued reading:

Mrs. Coronado is positive that he intends to take his life as he has discussed this before. Stated that they would never have to worry about it that he would go down near the bay to do it. Mrs. Coronado stated that one of her sons had talked to him Sunday and he was sober and told him the same thing so it was not the liquor talking. At this time he is on vacation from his job.

"What a fucked up way to spend your vacation," I said to the cat, who looked at me with sleepy eyes.

The final paragraph of the report revealed:

> This man has had no formal education and understands very little about children, he becomes very upset if things do not proceed the way he thinks they should.

I got up and filled another shot glass with tequila. "*Ayyyy,*" I exclaimed with a harsh voice, and repeated the action. I strutted back into the living room thinking about the primate next door, "I've wanted that asshole for a long time now." As I stood in front of the couch, I swiped at the papers on the coffee table and came up with the supplemental report:

> Reported her husband Ignacio leaving the house with a .38 Cal. pistol and is afraid he intends to take his life.
>
> Mrs. Coronado was questioned as to places where her husband spent his time. Stated he spent a lot of time on the rocks near the tunnel in Point Richmond. He has been known to associate *Mi Bar* on MacDonald Ave. These places were checked and also the Garden tract area out near the garbage dump. The Wonder Bar and George's Place was also checked failed to locate the man.
>
> Information has been passed on to the rest of the men in the Dept.

"Round up the usual suspects," I said to the cat. I laughed a harsh, bitter, snarling laugh. Then cried a deep, painful, mournful, cry. "*Ay, m'ijito, te quiero mucho,*" I reminisced, hearing my father's strong and soothing voice.

My eyes were now filled with tears, sweat, and the effects of alcohol. I focused on the coffee table and sardonically asked, "Now which bit of social realism have I not read?" I jabbed at the Deputy Coroner's Preliminary Report. I scanned the vital statistics, and my eyes were stopped by the heading "Nativity" with the blank next to it filled in with "Mexico." Underneath that, the "Occupation" blank was filled in with

"Laborer." "Do those two fucking words always go hand in hand?" I asked no one.

I drunkenly focused on the section titled "History." "Oh, good! We get to read some history, boys and girls," I lashed out to an imaginary classroom, or family:

> Mrs. Coronado states that her husband had spoken of suicide on many occasions the last time being Sunday 5-14-61. It was reported that he had been disturbed due to a domestic quarrel over finances. Alcohol had been a problem with Mr. Coronado and it's use seemed to deepen his melancholy. He left home about 2:45 P.M. 5-17-61 according to a neighbor. Mrs. Coronado had left to pick up her children at school and on her return found an open holster on the bed and 10 rounds of .38 cal. ammo gone. Her son, Roberto, tried to find Mr. Coronado and combed the area for the rest of the night. The San Pablo Police Dept. was notified and an all points was issued. The elder son continued his search this date and about 3:00 P.M. this date found Mr. Coronado in a vacant lot not far from his home. He notified the San Pablo Police. Mrs. Coronado was questioned by this deputy and she stated that she felt this was his own act and that there were no others involved. At this writing this deputy and police are of the same opinion.

"What the hell do you mean 'there were no others involved?'" I screamed. "What were we, *chorizo con huevos?*" "No," the sneering voice in my poisoned mind explained, "you were *chorizo* without the *huevos.*"

"¡Thanks a lot *Papacito!*" I cried out. "You left me at the hands of *mamá* and my sisters to raise me to be the weak man I've become! To study something stupid like English that doesn't mean shit today, and because of your stupid, dramatic abandonment, I've become a drunken, drug-abusing misfit."

I picked up the coffee table, and with a force that surprised me, I slammed it straight down to the floor. I laughed hysterically as shrapnel of cheap wood exploded around me. Imitating the voice of Bullwinkle, I said to the fleeing cat, "Don't know my own strength."

I staggered toward the kitchen for another drink, and fell to the floor. Lying face down, I pounded the floor with open palms. "Why didn't anybody ever tell me the real story? Why did I have to read it from the writing of cops who can't spell and don't know where to put a comma?"

As the lonely night turned into a new morning, José Alfredo sang about a drunk who arrives drunk asking for more tequila than he needs: *"Llegó borracho el borracho, pidiendo cinco tequilas...."*

## 36

It was difficult for me to learn English at school. I attribute much of that to the fact that I was suffused with my mother's language at home. My mother cursed me for making fun of her English, which was often. Sometimes she just called me a *condenado*, or *desgraciado*, or *jodón*. But when she really wanted to let me know who I was, she would say, *"¡hijo a la fregada madre que te parió!"* This one always struck me because I interpreted that exchange to mean "son of the useless mother that bore you!" I would duly respond with, "Now, Mom, don't talk that way about yourself."

*"¡Cabroncito!"* she would playfully reply.

My mother had an unusual way of expressing her affection, and she often did this in an imagistic and teasingly tough fashion. As I was growing up, she had a nickname for me that seemed to change as my physical appearance changed. I remember first being *ojos de tacuache* or "possum eyes." Later, as my personality revealed a perpetually frightened young boy, I became *cagias*, the intended meaning being "one who shits his pants in fear." When puberty began to inflate my body to a soft chubbiness, I became *timbón* or "kettledrum." During this time, whenever my mother was feeling especially endearing, I was *timboncito* or "little kettledrum."

"I do have a name, you know," I informed my mother one day. "You named me Ricardo Patricio Cásares Coronado, but you never use any of those names."

"Well, son, you know I call you those other names because I love you," she explained.

"And you named me Patricio because I was born on St. Patrick's Day?" I asked. Before she could explain, I threw in, "What if I had been born on Groundhog Day?"

As my propensity to devour any edibles in the house became all too obvious to my mother, and I seemed to exceed what she thought was a normal and satiating amount of food, she would address me as *tragón* or, as she defined the term in her English, "eater guy." Often during this time, she used *tragón* interchangeably with *brutón* or "brutish guy." As I matured, my full head of hair inspired her to consider a new name for me: *perro peludo*, or "hairy dog."

My stepfather also had terms of affection hurled at him. He was many things to my mother: *ojos de chino*, Chinese eyes; *cara de chango*, monkey face; and *piernas de guajalote*, turkey legs.

I loved my mother's imagery when it was applied to other people, and I was amazed at how others looked to her. There was the time we went to sell our junk at the *pulga*, the flea market, and when we finally had our wares neatly displayed on the table, many people began to approach us to examine our inventory. My mother whispered, "*Aquí vienen todos con sus manos de cangrejos,*" as she described the crab-like hands of people attempting to poke, pinch, and pilfer something. When a graying and wavy-haired man insisted that my mother sell him a used set of kitchen utensils for half of what she was asking, she expressed her annoyance to me by saying, "*Ese ladrón con cabello de repollo....*" I laughed as she folded her arms in a pose of indignation and vilified, "the thief who has hair like cabbage."

Of course, my mother was proud of her imagination. She would explain, "You see, son, and I didn't went to school, *nunca.*"

Once, as my mother was vacuuming the living room rug, she told my wife, who was sitting in a chair, to move her feet. "*Mueve tus chalupas,*" she said.

"What does that mean?" my wife asked.

"It means, 'move your boats,'" I explained.

Another time, as my mother was trying to sell my wife some used shoes, she asked her, "What size are your *patas*?"

"What are *petas*?" my wife asked.

"It's *patas*," I corrected, and I suggested that we look it up in a Spanish/English dictionary. "Look up p-a-t-a," I instructed.

"Here it is!" my wife exclaimed.

"What does it mean?" I asked as my mother began to chuckle.

"It says, 'paw, foot, or hoof,' my wife answered, and continued, "and then in brackets it says 'of animals.'"

"Yes," I responded, "paws and hoofs usually are of animals." I went into my lecture mode. "If she had wanted to know the size of your feet, she would have asked 'What size are your, *pies*.' But because of the enormity of those skis you call—"

"Okay, okay!" my wife interrupted. "I think I get the gist of what you're saying."

"*Mejor que se vaya con herraduras*," my mom commented, and shook her head and laughed. And then for my wife's benefit, "You would be better with horseshoes!"

Many of those who were fortunate enough to engage in an English conversation with my mother often experienced new insights and philosophies. When my mother was lamenting to a neighbor about crooked politicians, she sighed and mused, "Well, if you can't beat them, enjoy them." When I first heard this idiomatic twist, I had the impulse to correct her. But then I thought about the positive message—much less cynical than the original—in her version, and I concluded, "Yes, she is truly a thinker."

One time my mother wanted me to go next door to tell the neighbor to come and knock on our door when she was ready to go shopping. I was willing, but poorly prepared. The neighbor spoke no English, and I was re-learning how to speak Spanish.

"How do you say 'knock' in Spanish?" I asked my mom.

She looked at me quizzically, tilted her head slightly, and then responded, "*Pues, knockiar*."

"*¡Knockiar?*" I asked with surprised doubt. "That's not how you say 'knock' in Spanish. Come on, Mom."

"What do you means that's not how you say 'knock' in Spanish? Why do you ask me if you don't believe me?"

"No, really, Mom," I answered, "you're using an English word with a Spanish ending, *knockiar* isn't even a word. You have two languages mixed up."

For a few moments she studied me with a glaring intensity. "I bet you if you go tell Carmelita that I want her to *knockiar* when she's ready to go, she will understand you." She thrust a chubby hand out at me to secure a bet.

"I'm not going to bet you, Mom," I said. "I just want to know if that's a word, and where you got it from."

"What do you mean, where did I get that word from? It's a word all of us know."

"Can you conjugate the word?" I asked.

"¿*Cómo*?" she asked, looking perplexed. "Can I do what with that word?"

"Can you conjugate it? You know, are there different forms of the word like: *yo knockio, tú knockias, usted, él, o ella knockia, nosotros knockiamos,* and *ustedes, ellos, o ellas knockian*?"

She had enough of my questions, and decided to deliver the message to Carmelita herself. As she headed for the front door, she turned to me and said, "Son, if you want to learn to speak Spanish better, you have to *cuitear* asking such *tonto* questions like if *knockiar* is a word."

There was a time when my mother went through a stage of inquisitiveness and really showed a desire to learn. "¿*Qué quiere decir,* chee wee?" she asked.

I stared at her for a moment as my brain scanned its database in an attempt to match what it was that my mother had heard in English and was now contorting into her own genuine mode of expression. "Hmmm, chee wee," I pondered out loud as I felt a form of the answer appearing on the terminal in my head. "I think you might mean, gee whiz," I offered hesitantly.

And before I could provide a definition, she exclaimed, "¡*Ah, sí!* That's what I hear, chee wee."

My mother's confusion with language forced me into my own confusion with words, idioms, correct word usage and meanings, and it further forced me into rationalizing definitions and explanations as best I could.

"Who is Mike?" she asked one day, catching me completely off guard.

"Mike?" I responded in earnest confusion. "Mike who?"

"*Pues*, that's what I'm asking you, *hombre*," she retorted as her eagerness to learn made her snappy.

"I don't know what you mean," I replied, tilting my head slightly and offering an ear as if I hadn't heard correctly.

"You know," she urged, "Mike, when people say, 'for the love of Mike.'"

I suppressed the laughter until my face burst like an overblown balloon.

"Okay, *fregón*, laugh at your poor *mamá*. When I die, you will say, '*Ay, Dios*, forgive me for making fun of my mother.' And then you feel sorry," she prophesied.

"I'm sorry now," I responded, realizing I would have to be careful with my sensitive student.

I thought about my opening comments and started, "Well, you see, it's a saying, *un dicho*. And what it really says, is 'for the love of *might*.'" I emphasized the word connoting power and repeated *might* and dipped my head forward anticipating comprehension.

Her green eyes gleamed as she studied me in an attempt to discern if her son was teaching her or taunting her. She shriveled her face in confusion and asked about the foolishness of my explanation, "*¿Qué quiere decir esa tontería?*"

"Well," I carefully continued, not wanting to lose my student, "the word *might* is used here to mean *power*." I suddenly realized that further explanation would be necessary as the process of teaching and learning began to take its tortuous route. "You know the word *might* is another word for *power*, and *might* in 'for the love of might,' means *power*, or *poder*," I explained.

"*No entiendo*. I don't get it," she relented.

"Okay, now look," I attempted. "Let's change it to 'for the love of *power*,'" and I waited a few seconds to ensure that she was still with me. "Now, don't people like *power*?" I asked, and went on not waiting for an answer. "You know, you are always complaining about the *condenado* politicians and how they don't care for us and that they have too much *power*, or *might*." I was feeling good about what I had just expressed and the infection grew. "Don't you think those guys love the *power* or *might* they have?" I asked, trying to engage my pupil.

"Well," she slowly began, "yes, but I don't—"

I cut her off at the point of confusion and continued, "So, when someone says 'for the love of might,' they are using that saying as if they are frustrated because someone did something to them because they are more powerful or they *love might*, or *power*." I raised my eyebrows hoping that I had reached my singular student.

"Where does that comes from?" she asked, dismissing the new learning as mere silliness.

"I don't know, but do you get it?" I asked. "Do you under-stand what I just explained?"

"Yes, I guess so," she relented.

I looked at her as she showed obvious disillusionment at the lesson. She looked at me curiously, and her face grew luminous with thought. "Okay, *listo*," she began again in a challenging tone, "and now you're gonna tell your *pobre mamá* that Pete's not Pete. Huh?"

"Pete who?" I asked, feeling frustrated and spent.

"You know, Pete in 'for Pete's sake.'"

## 37

I sat in my dark office doing some light reading and waiting for my obligatory office hour to pass. I knew I would have no visitors as the Developmental English students whom I taught were not even mildly interested in the things I might have to offer. I didn't blame them really. Many years prior, before I was charged with teaching college composition, I was a student in Developmental English and had the same indifferent attitude towards education.

I tried to make English interesting. I even tried to be a bit of a performer in the act of my teaching, hoping I could maintain contact throughout two classes of seventy-five minute periods two times a week. I cared deeply about my students. After all, for the most part we had come from the same place. On the other hand, I refused to let my concern and enthusiasm coddle these very young adults.

The knock on the door surprised me. For a few seconds I wondered which one it could be. I thought about Jamal, who wanted to be a lawyer. "No, it can't be him," I said to myself. "He thinks he's already a lawyer and school is just a formality." Shannon's face flashed in my mind. "No, it's not her," I quickly concluded. "She was in Honors English in high school and it was, in her words, 'Totally unfair that I have to be in your class, Mr. Coronado.'" So in her mind, she definitely did not need my help, although she really did. Thoc's shy presence timidly entered my thoughts as I beamed like a proud parent. "God, she's a good student," I said to myself, admiring such sincerity and seriousness of effort. "And English is her second language! It could be her." As I got up to see who the petitioner was, I thought about Aureliano. "No, it's not him either. He doesn't trust me for some reason."

I opened the door and was greeted by one of the three tutors whom I supervised. Brian was an eager and aggressive tutor—he had declared this to me when we first met. He was a senior and would be graduating at the end of the semester with highest honors. He had already been accepted in the Master's program to study English literature at a major university.

"Hi, Rick," Brian cordially greeted me.

"Hi, Brian," I said. "How are you?"

"I'm fine, thank you. Do you have a few minutes?"

"Sure, my office hour is usually composed of sixty uninterrupted minutes of profound meditation," I answered, attempting to inject a little levity into the budding conversation.

Brian stood for a moment and then announced his business. "I need to talk to you about a paper."

"Oh, well sit down," I invited, "A paper of yours or one of the students'?"

"Well, it's about one of the students' papers."

"Oh?" I said as I slightly tilted my head indicating I was ready to listen.

"Yeah," Brian slowly began, "it's about Yolanda's paper."

I thought about Yolanda for a moment. We had a good working relationship, and she understood completely what was expected of her. Yolanda had only been speaking English for four years, and she modestly agreed with me that, yes indeed, it was quite impressive that in only four years she was now in a college English class. Her writing was coming along. She still had problems with verb tense, and the use of articles, and much of her expression, although thought-provoking, was still quite awkward.

"Rick," Brian continued, "you know what you should do? You should give two grades for each paper, one for mechanics and one for content."

I was a bit taken aback by what seemed to me to be pure effrontery. "Why? What's the problem?"

"Well," Brian slowly started and then accelerated, "I can't help but think that you are lacking in appreciation of what these students are writing. Rick, you just do not seem to appreciate the poetics of a sentence fragment, and I am deeply concerned." Brian came up for air as I nervously played with the hair on the back of my neck. "Here's Yolanda's paper," he said. "Let's look at this first paragraph,"

> When I get alone I feel like I want to be alone with
> Nature. Nature is so piecefull and beutifull and nice
> to be around. That is why we call her Mother Nature,
> because of the things I have just mention. There a
> place I go when I want to be with Mother Nature. The
> Duck Pond. Over by the picnic area on this campus.

Brian read the paper slowly, stopping to emote at the beautiful passages of what he perceived to be the communion of writing.

"Now, Rick," Brian lectured, "all you did here is slash and burn this paper. You failed to notice the poetics of what this person is trying to share with us. And then, at the end, when she wrote that beautiful poem, you did not make one comment about the poem."

I felt the anger rise inside me. Granted, I had only been a teacher for two years, and part-time at that, but I had received commendable student and peer evaluations. I kept in close contact with the composition director in an effort to become completely involved in my new profession and to engage in current dialogue about who was being taught what. My anger also contained another twist as I thought about Brian and his unsullied life. Both of his parents were college graduates and corporate executives. I thought about my own parents who had been migrant farm workers and had taught all of their children "the meaning of hard work." Brian was not familiar with the soiled backgrounds from where most of my students came. I thought it strange that he should purport to know what was best for inner-city, immigrant, and low-income students as he prepared for an advanced degree at an Ivy League institution.

"And here I got my M.A. at a little-known state college," I thought to myself, and I began to resent the social classes of education and institutions. Insecurity and doubt were now beginning to add to the negative feelings that were developing in my mind.

I looked at Brian as he took a brief hiatus and waited for my explanation. "I don't evaluate creative writing," I said in an effort to excuse myself from my lack of poetic appreciation. I decided to go full-force with my method, while at the same time feeling a mounting resentment for the position in which I had allowed myself to be placed.

Brian had more, and he interpreted my solitary comment to be my only response. "Well, let's read the poem, Rick," he suggested. He cleared his throat and passionately read the poem to me:

> Nature gives us too much times;
> We have times to be born;
> We have times to be die;
> We have times to learn;
> We have times not to learn;
> We have times to help others;
> We have times to others to help us;
> We have times to be with Mother Nature;
> We have times not to be with Mother Nature;

As Brian read the first few lines, I interrupted with "It sounds like Ecclesiastes." Brian looked at me with a trace of confident confusion and dismissed my comment with "I don't know that one." He continued reading, but before he finished the poem, I calmly told Brian to stop and to proceed with the literary criticism.

"Rick, you are really missing the point here. This student writes something as sensitive and feeling as this, and you didn't even comment on it. I can't help but think that you are doing a tremendous disservice to these kids. And certainly you aren't going to win any popularity contests with them."

Inwardly I snapped, but I put forth my greatest effort not to reveal the rage that was rioting in my mind. I stared directly into his eyes and calmly gave a defense of my method.

"Brian, this is not a creative writing class, and the university does not pay me to appreciate sentence fragments. Also, I'm not trying to win any popularity contests; I don't teach to be liked. I realize the efforts these students put into their work. But largely what we need to work on is at the syntactical and paragraphical levels. There are many problems with subject-verb agreement, run-on sentences, you know, the stuff that's no fun. But we've got to do it. When these students get into a real English composition class, one that counts for real units and isn't just credit/no-credit, the instructors there are not going to be concerned with the poetics of a sentence fragment. I understand it sounds insensitive, but to me that is the reality of what my students will face next semester, and I want them to be prepared for real things. It's a rude awakening for many students and I don't like rudeness." I felt good about what I had just explained, when a question popped into my mind. "So tell me, Brian, how did you get Yolanda's paper anyway? And why isn't she here to discuss her own work with me?"

Brian showed the slightest kink in his intellectual armor as he looked at me with an embarrassed simper. "Yolanda looked so sad," he said, "and I asked her what was wrong. She said it was the grade she received on her essay."

"It was a C," I said blankly. "What did she think she deserved?" Brian ignored my question and started to duck into another intellectual alley when I stopped him curtly and said, "Brian, that was not a rhetorical question. What did Yolanda think she deserved for her essay?"

"Well, she just said she'll try harder on the next paper," he answered.

"Why did she give you her paper, Brian?" I was now imagining that Brian's simpering countenance was sprouting donkey ears as a light flush of blood continued to fill his face.

"Well, she didn't give me her paper," he slowly began. "I asked her for it and told her I would talk to you about it."

"Do you plan on being her spokesman during the rest of her college career?" I asked, and did not wait for an answer, "And why just Yolanda's paper? You also have Rodrigo, Irma, Debbie, Duane, and Phan. They all had sad and surprised looks on their faces after I returned their papers to them. I am perceptive enough to see those things. I expect Duane wants to kick my ass for what I wrote on his paper, but I can't and won't give anything away." Brian was now looking at the floor as he reloaded for more discussion.

I decided that I'd had enough, and I expressed that this symposium had now ended. "Brian, it's time for you to leave," I invited. "I want you to seriously consider talking to the composition director, Dr. Edwards, or even with the new professor who is a rhetorician and will be the next composition director. Tell them all about me and my ways. Especially if you are truly concerned with the disservice that I am heaping on my students." I stood up and opened the door for Brian.

"I can't be anymore blunt but to say that you are really damaging these kids, Rick," he offered as he walked out.

"They were already damaged as kids. Now they are adults, and there is still plenty of time to help them meet whatever goals they set. What they don't need is the mixed messages from an upper-class liberal polity that oozes to the disenfranchised that their sentence fragments are poetic while they continue to plod in a white man's system of education." And I added as he was walking down the hallway, "I'll call Dr. Edwards and tell him you will be in to see him."

I gathered my books and papers and threw them into my briefcase. I walked to my car thinking about what I was doing as an instructor and how I was doing it. "Who needs this crap? I should just quit and go back to the factory. Why is it that those who have always had it, think they know what is best for those who never have?"

## 38

"Well, I guess this is it, Honey," I said to my wife as we sat on the floor in a nearly empty apartment holding each other's hands. Our cars were packed with what few belongings we had left. I was resigned to what was slowly happening, but that resignation meant for me that it was time to quit—everything.

"We'll be okay," she said. "Let's just keep hanging in there. You never know what will happen."

"Yes, I do know what will happen!" I shot back. "My stupid life will continue in a way that situates me on the sidelines while the rest of the world rushes by on their way to success. I'm tired, Honey. It's all been so futile. I worked hard to get my Master's degree, thinking I could just go out and get a teaching position somewhere in this great, golden state of diversity that keeps churning out the messages that there is a need for more ethnic faculty. It's bullshit rhetoric. And then to make sure they've covered their own privileged asses, those in charge, those with places in the world, extend that language in the rejection letters they send out. Look at the one I received yesterday from that small junior college in northern California:

> We have closely considered your application package, and after considering the applications of many fine applicants, our selection committee has chosen a candidate whose abilities and qualifications are more appropriately suited to our requirements for Instructor of English. We are pleased to announce the appointment of Erlinda Hernandez.

What this letter is really conveying in that last sentence is that the school or the district wants, especially for people of my ilk, to know that not only did they hire an ethnic person, they hired an ethnic woman. The letter might as well end with 'So there Chicanito!' I have not received in the almost one hundred rejection letters that I already have, any statement about who the lucky person is who was given the positions I had applied for. Why do they do stupid stuff like that? What do they think? That I'm going to call the ACLU?

"You know, Honey, I've been teaching for two years part-time, hoping a full-time gig would eventually come up, and now I've been laid off from that. I have sent out over two dozen applications a year for the past three years, and I don't have enough goddamn experience? All of these applications and job descriptions say that preference will be given to those who show an understanding and sensitivity to students of different cultural, economic, ethnic, and academic backgrounds. I just want for once to experience that preference and privilege. You know, a lot of what success means is who you know and who you blow, then your qualifications and abilities might be considered. I want the playing field to be just a little more even. I realize there are a bunch of people ahead of me with more experience, but I didn't expect that we would have to sell all of our stuff just to keep living and paying bills. I thought the way the story went was you went to college, you got a respectable, well-paying job, and then you joined the middle class. Having that presumption corrected, I've even shown a willingness to work at any kind of job outside of teaching. But nobody else wants to hire me because prospective employers keep insisting that as soon as a teaching position becomes available, I'll leave. I tried to tell them that there are no teaching jobs in California, or in the country for that matter, especially for people new to the profession. I refer to the state budget and the educational sliver that comes out of that budget which is always in the news, and they just say, 'Oh, yeah, I have heard something about that.' And that's it. I never get called back for another interview or a job."

"But, Ricky, I still have my job," my wife said as she tried to soothe and show me the good things about our life together. "We just need to move to a cheaper place."

"Yeah, I know" I said, "there's a beautiful little dump down by the race track that we might be able to afford. It's already furnished with its own hypodermic needles, and the exterior is contemporary graffiti. The neighborhood crack dealer lives on the corner. What else can you ask for? And while you work, I can stay at home filling out applications and writing. I can be the next Karl Marx, huh?"

"Come on, Honey," she said. "We're going to pull—"

"Bullshit!" I yelled. "That's it, Honey. I'm leaving. You don't need to live like this. You can marry one of those lawyers who's always hitting up on you. Lawyers like to mess around with their hired help. At least get some money out of it. That's more than you've been able to see from me."

"Where will you go?"

"Who cares?" I said. "It doesn't matter. I'll just drive around looking for work or a place to die. Maybe I'll stand out on a street corner with a sign that says 'Will teach English for food.' Mónica said they can take one of us. You can go live there until you find somebody successful."

"I have found somebody successful!" my wife exclaimed. "You just haven't been lucky."

"But why haven't I been lucky, Honey?" I asked, feeling foiled by the events of existence. "What have I done wrong? What am I doing wrong? I feel like I'm being punished for something. I'm trying to understand my situation either cosmically, spiritually, philosophically, and I just don't get it. I must have been a real asshole in a previous life, and I'm paying for it now. I worked at a factory while I got an education, graduated with high marks—," and I couldn't finish as I choked on my own frustration. "This is more than I can take," I continued. "There are people who have done less and are doing much better than we are. It's embarrassing. I feel foolish for having pursued a college degree. You know, you really pay for pursuing your passion."

"I'll give you that, honey," she admitted. "It is confusing. No, you didn't do anything wrong. And yes, there are many others who are doing better with less effort and education. And I can see how it can be embarrassing, but that doesn't mean you give up."

"It *can* mean that, Honey," I said, and offered an explanation. "You see it's really like an extension of the legacy my dad left me with his suicide. Since I don't have what it takes to commit instant suicide, I constantly commit many other types of slower symbolic suicide. I kill my relations with my family. I kill my prior work life by leaving the assembly line angry and bitter with no chance of a resurrection. I think I

tried for years to subconsciously kill myself by taking numer-
ous drugs at one time, never caring to know what it was I was
swallowing. And now, I'm killing this marriage. It's like I'm
holding myself hostage. If life doesn't meet my demands, the
hostage will die. If I ever do get drunk or stoned enough,
maybe *I* will kneel down in a field of tall grass and point my
father's gun at my heart. Too bad I didn't have a son to carry
on the family tradition, huh?"

"How can you just leave? Don't you even care about—,"
she pleaded. But I interrupted her before she could hurt my
heart with things that might seem like truisms. Like the
solid, profound relationship we really did have. The careful
consideration we showed to each other when one of us, usually me, was feeling manic and moody. The respectful tender-
ness we had for each other when we made love. The silly little
nicknames and personal language that only we shared. I did-
n't want to think about these things, because now the over-
whelming feelings of losing my home, my job, and any trace of
esteem I might still conjure were raping my mind.

"No, I don't! Don't you understand?" I stressed. "I'm no
good at life. I'm still wondering what it would be like to own a
home. I'm over thirty years old and I have never owned property. I've always lived from paycheck to paycheck, all my life.
And if that's all honest work gets you, then I've had enough. I
don't want to do this anymore."

I was silent for a few moments while the dementia began
a complete consumption of my mind. Taking hold of my wife's
left hand, I stared sadly at her wedding ring and calmly said,
"It shouldn't seem so unusual. There are a lot of us in the
world like this. We do it every day. We get younger and younger. Really, we help to balance the environment. Our deaths
help the unemployment statistics go down. We get buried, and
an organic symbiosis is created between human and earth.
That's what rest in peace really means.

"Look, Honey, I've just got to leave. I need to go some
place different and try to figure some things out. I'm going to
drive around. If I find something, I'll call or write. You take
care, Honey." I kissed her quickly as we both cried, and I ran
out of the empty home.

To pacify my infected mind, I thought about how my wife
would at least be living with my sister and her family. And
together, with a few incomes, they could all live comfortably

and not have the parasitic strain of my presence. I really had no idea of where I would go. Flashes of those places where I used to live when I was a young boy and a younger man fanned before me. But returning to any of those places would be like a dog returning to eat its own vomit. I would just drive somewhere, anywhere; it no longer mattered. If I decided to stay alive, I could sleep in my car, maybe even keep trying to look for work. "Maybe," I thought to myself as I drove away, "I'll be as brave as my dad was when he decided his own life should end."

## 39

The six cups of coffee only made me a more alert drunk. I had staggered into the all-night cafe after a period of all-night drinking. As I sat alone at a booth, I wondered why my life had taken the twists and turns it had. I wondered what I had done wrong. And I blamed everything on God.

I was homeless—at least in the traditional sense. I did have a small car to sleep in. And I got my food by doing odd jobs, and when really desperate, by stealing things from grocery stores. Occasionally, I visited a campground to shower, but most of the time, I remained dirty. It just didn't seem right that I could not find work after having attended school for eight years, earning three degrees, and teaching part-time for a couple of years. My training wasn't producing anything. My impressive letters of recommendation, stellar evaluations, ambitious transcripts and diplomas meant very little. But much of the country was experiencing this. And the only state I had ever lived in, *my California*, was hit especially hard. It was the end-of-the-century depression years, just like the ones my mother had told me she had survived about sixty years earlier. But those in power didn't like the word "depression," and an underlying political predilection was that the have-nots simply weren't trying hard enough.

"I studied the wrong stuff in school," I said to myself, watching the whirlpool of black coffee as I stirred in more sugar. To make my miserable life complete, the tightly knit unit that had been a marriage was unraveling, and I dangled in the world alone.

As I walked to my car-home, I thought about how meaningless life seemed. "You're just picking on me," I said to God, who never explicitly responded or answered to my needs. "And that's no way for a Heavenly Father to treat his spiritual son. That's child abuse."

I drove down the deserted avenue. I squinted at my watch and thought about how the sun would soon rise to illuminate yet another nondescript day for me. I dreamed about teaching and the day I would get the call or read the letter that said a secure teaching position was being offered. My fancy ran to images of returning to my wife and family in professional triumph. In my illusion, we hugged and were happy that I had finally arrived. My drunken daydreaming showed me comfort, security, and the ability to help others. As my imagination took me to other worlds on the same planet, I yearned for real success.

My mobile home sped along the avenue. In an explosive instant, I was shockingly awakened from my dream state by a thunderous crash that violently shoved my body into the steering wheel.

"Holy shit!" I exclaimed as I saw the enormous palm tree standing directly in front of my shattered windshield. My car had a v-shape carved into it as it hugged the tree. The engine groaned as smoke drifted into the cool dark morning air.

I shifted into reverse and stomped the accelerator. The tree slowly released its seemingly magnetic hold. I shook my head clear of residual self-pity, shifted into drive, and was back on the street.

"I'm in big fucking trouble now," I said to myself as I desperately forced the dying vehicle to go on. I drove through two red lights with determination and purpose. As I turned the corner, not knowing where I was headed, a high-fenced yard with a weathered sign that read "Burrow's Auto Wrecking," loomed as a dead end.

I parked in front of the sign and got out to inspect my body. My right hand and arm bled from impressive scrapes, and my ribs and chest thumped with pain. My forehead bled slowly, and my knees were stiff with the effects of the hard impact. I hunched over holding my ribs and chest and thought to myself that I must look like Quasimodo.

"You don't look too good," a voice observed. I turned to see an old man opening the gates to Burrow's Auto Wrecking as he emerged from a graveyard of metal corpses.

"You're right about that," I moaned as I looked at the violence that was the front of my vehicle.

"So how much do you want for your wreck?" he asked.

"Huh?" I said, not sure if I had heard him correctly.

"Well, didn't you bring that thing here to see what you could get for it?" he explained. He didn't seem to realize or care that the damage to the car was as new as the day that was emerging.

I thought about nothing for a few perplexing seconds, and a voice inside of me weakly responded with "Yes, I did."

"Well, come on in. Have a cup of coffee while we take care of the paperwork. You do have title to the car, don't you?" he asked as he led me to a dark and dirty office.

A Doberman pinscher stood in the doorway and stared at me before coming forward to sniff my presence. He licked at the blood on my arm as I sat hunched and leaning. "Satan, leave him alone!" the old man ordered, pushing the dog away from me. "Now, cars like yours aren't in big demand, but the back of it is in good condition and the seats look good. I can give you three hundred dollars for it."

"I'll take it," I responded, and signed the little square piece of paper that transferred the responsibility of ownership from me to him.

"Here, take these, too," he offered, placing three aspirins on the counter in front of me. He chuckled slightly and said "You wrapped that thing around something solid. What'd you hit, a tree?"

"Yes, a palm tree."

"Did you do that on purpose?"

I looked at his objective but kind eyes and after a moment of silence I asked, "Did I wreck my car on purpose?"

"No, did you hit a palm tree on Palm Sunday on purpose?" And he chuckled some more as he sifted through a rusty filing cabinet packed with the misfortune of others.

I hobbled down the street and thought about returning to my wife for some familiar comfort. "But will she take me back?" I asked myself. "Why should she? You ran out on her when she told you to stick with it. You're a pitiful fair-weather fan, you know that?" Later that morning, I made my way to a bus depot where I called my wife before boarding a busy bus.

As my wife helped me into her car, she told me there was a letter for me that had been lost in the mail. "It arrived about a week ago, but the postmark is dated two weeks earlier than that. It's from some school."

I slept for many hours after we arrived at my sister's house. When I awoke, the letter was on the nightstand. The return address indicated one of the many universities to which I had applied in the hopes of being accepted as a Ph.D candidate, thereby securing a trace of purpose and validation in my life. "Another academic Dear John letter," I thought to myself as I tore open the envelope. I read with little enthusiasm:

Dear Mr. Coronado:

We are pleased to inform you that your application has been reviewed and you have been selected by our review committee as a candidate to the Ph.D program for which you have applied. In addition, we will be awarding you a minority teaching fellowship. It is important that you contact Dr. Ashe as soon as possible to inform him of your decision in accepting this offer.

I read the letter many times and was unsure as to how to react. "Of course I'll accept, I guess," I said to myself. I was tentative and nervous and wondered what was going on with my life.

"Why are You putting me through all of this?" I asked God as I lay in bed. "Why are You making things so confusing? Couldn't You just have given me a full-time permanent teaching position somewhere and let me go on with my simple little life? What did I do to You?"

I thought about my past and my future and all the things I had done in an attempt to negate my own existence. I realized I still understood very little. "Okay, if that's the way You want it, I'll go along with You."

I recuperated for a few weeks while my wife continued to work. We mentally conditioned ourselves for our move to a place we had never been before and traced lines on a map that would guide us to a dot in the desert. After I was physically able to earn some odd-job money and we borrowed even more, my wife and I packed our truck and headed for the University of the Southwest, which would be my home for the next few years.

We drove a right angle through endless, flat miles of desert, heading south for hours and then east for an eternity. "Didn't the Joads do something like this, except in the opposite direction?" I joked as we descended into a slight valley that housed the university.

As we scanned the newspaper looking for a place to live, I thought about my plans to visit the campus as soon as possible, even though I had a few weeks before school was to begin.

Faculty members welcomed me, and after enjoying light and friendly conversation, I decided to visit the library to see where I would be spending much of my time. I asked a student where the library was, and he informed me that there were two. "Do you want the business and science library or the arts and humanities library?"

As I slowly walked toward the arts and humanities library, I read the class offerings for the upcoming fall semester. With an obscuring penumbra, the shade of a huge building crept into my space. When I looked up, my eyes were met and my senses were seized with the glory of many young palm trees in two neat and mated rows standing like eternal partners. I stopped and stared, my mouth agape, a series of cold shudders running up and down my body.

"Holy shit! I don't believe You," I said stunned. As I walked past the trees, I stopped and looked up into the clear blue southwestern sky, winked, and promised to do my best.

---

*Colorín colorado, este cuento se ha acabado.*